## "LOOK OUT," JARED SAID.

The woman's head snapped up and she stared at him. For a long, electric moment, their eyes met and Jared had the absurd thought that she could see all the way down into his soul.

"Don't worry," he said. She had the look of a doe trapped in the headlights, which was ridiculous. What could he, mild-mannered physician and volleyball player, do to her, kick-ass princess? "I'm here to rescue you."

Her lips twitched at that and she sidled toward him, then dashed past him as he came forward to meet her, turning left out the door. He could hear her running lightly and damned quickly.

"Hey!" he yelled and took off after her. Blessed—or cursed—with a Texan-sized curiosity bump, he had to catch her. She could tell him why there had been a fight, who the unconscious man was, her name, and if she was free for dinner any night this week. This year. She was the most intriguing woman—certainly the most beautiful—he'd ever seen.

More from MaryJanice Davidson

*Doing It Right*

*Drop Dead, Gorgeous!*

*Hello, Gorgeous!*

*Really Unusual Bad Boys*

*The Royal Mess*

*The Royal Pain*

*The Royal Treatment*

And look for her stories in these anthologies:

*Bad Boys with Expensive Toys*

*How to Be a "Wicked" Woman*

*Perfect for the Beach*

*Valentine's Day Is Killing Me*

Published by Kensington Publishing Corporation

# Doing It Right

## MaryJanice Davidson

**BRAVA**

KENSINGTON PUBLISHING CORP.

http://www.kensingtonbooks.com

*For all the readers who were willing to buy this hard-to-find e-book for hundreds of dollars. I, personally, don't think any book (certainly not one of mine) is worth hundreds of dollars, so I asked Brava to publish it in paperback. It was my editor's brilliant idea to reprint* Thief of Hearts *as well as a sequel (in novella form) in one paperback anthology; the smallish single title plus a follow-up novella, a novel (heh) idea that I immediately pounced on. So this is for Kate Duffy, too.*

# Acknowledgments

As always, writing the book is easy. Editing it, editing it again, checking and double-checking contracts, checking galleys, thinking up flap copy, designing the cover, marketing it, and selling it is hard. So, many thanks to the unsung heroes of publishing, all of whom are busy making me rich.

Thanks to the fans who tirelessly track down my backlist. If not for all the requests for this anthology, it wouldn't have been done. I hope it was worth the wait! (Not to mention the $14.00.)

Thanks to my husband, Anthony, who reads everything I write and isn't afraid to tell me when something sucks, the bum. And thanks to my darling children, who are adept at entertaining themselves when Mommy is on deadline, and who only bother me when something is on fire.

Thanks also to my wonderful Yahoo group, a gang of readers who are unfailingly supportive and considerate, both of me and of each other. It's the nicest group on the web . . . Check 'em out at *http://groups.yahoo.com/group/maryjanice/*.

Th-th-that th-th-that th-th-that's all, folks!

"The thief steals from himself. The swindler swindles himself."
—Ralph Waldo Emerson, *Compensation*

"In a way, I'm a thief just the same as you are. But I won't sell you hope when there ain't any."
—Charles Schnee, U.S. screenwriter

"Nowadays the thief cannot be distinguished from his victim. Neither has any valuable objects on him."
—Karl Kraus, *Beim Wort genommen*

Betty White: "And if you watch one minute [of PBS] without contributing, you're a thief! A common thief!"
PBS rep: "Okay, Betty White, calm down."
Betty White: "I'm sorry. It's just that these thieves make me so damn mad. You know who you are . . . *thieves!*"
—*The Simpsons*, "Missionary: Impossible"

# Author's Note

Stealing is wrong. So is vigilantism. But sometimes you gotta do what you gotta do.

# Contents

# THIEF OF HEARTS

# Chapter 1

Dr. Jared Dean hated being interrupted more than just about anything in the world. So he was annoyed when he heard the crash of something falling over in the chart room. *For heaven's sake,* he thought darkly, scrawling orders for one of the seven patients he'd admitted that evening, *just put the charts back in their rows, you guys. Don't play keep-away with them.*

"What's going on in there?" Shari, one of the RN floats, asked without looking up from restocking the meds cabinet.

"The guys have too much time on their hands," Jared said, writing *NO NARCOTICS!!!!!!!* in Mrs. O'Leary's chart and underlining it twice. Mrs. O'Leary ("Like the lady with the cow, honey.") was a frequent visitor to the ER. To all the emergency rooms in the city, actually. She was in her late forties, impeccably groomed, ridiculously rich, and hopelessly hooked on Demerol and Vicodin. Jared had been trying to get her into a drug treatment program for two years, to no avail. Mrs. O'Leary thought drug addicts were smelly street people who skin-popped heroin (not that she knew, or used, the phrase "skin-popped"), not grand dames of society who contributed six figures to charity every year.

"Can't blame them for horsing around. Third shift can be a snoozer." He glanced at his watch—three in the morning, groan—and swallowed a yawn.

"Maybe we should threaten to sic the A.A. on them," Shari joked.

Jared snorted. He didn't believe in Santa Claus, the Tooth Fairy, a balanced federal budget, city buses that ran according to the bus schedule, or vigilantes who ran around at night righting wrongs. The newspapers had been whispering about the A.A.'s activities for almost a decade.

"At least the clerks aren't pulling this crap during first shift," Shari added, shoving a hank of her strawberry blond hair out of her eyes. "You know how those morning weenies can get."

Jared was about to answer her when there was a dull thump. The sharp crack of someone slamming against the window brought him to his feet. He moved past an open-mouthed Shari, headed for the chart room at a dead run, and fairly leapt through the doorway, ready to start chewing some ass . . . or kicking some.

Instead, he stood there with his mouth open. Nothing he'd seen in his years as a med student, intern, and ER resident prepared him for the sight of a startlingly beautiful woman engaged in a vicious hand-to-hand battle with the largest man he'd ever seen.

And winning.

She was stunning. Petite—her assailant was well over a foot taller—and delicately built, with small hands and feet. Her white blond hair was skinned back into a French knot at the nape of her neck. She looked like a princess, one who could pour tea or break your nose, depending on how you addressed her. She was dressed in dark colors—black turtleneck, black leggings, dark shoes—which accentuated her fair skin and hair. Exertion had brought a delicate flush to her features.

Her assailant wasn't nearly so attractive—dirty blond hair shaved close to his skull, thick black eyebrows that met in the center of his forehead, fists the size of bowling balls, a nose that had been broken at least twice. Thick lips skinned back from his teeth as he snarled wordlessly at the woman and sent a punch whistling toward her wide-eyed face.

Jared opened his mouth to shout a warning . . . and the woman deftly blocked the punch, twisted the man around without letting go of his arm, and slammed him, facedown, on the table. Jared winced at the *pop* the man's shoulder made coming out of its socket.

The man howled curses, which were abruptly cut off as the woman grabbed a fold of skin at the nape of his neck and slammed his head into the table.

Silence.

"Look out," Jared said, finally able to articulate. The woman's head snapped up and she stared at him. For a long, electric moment, their eyes met and Jared had the absurd thought that she could see all the way down into his soul. Her mouth popped open in a small *o* and she gasped, a quick intake of breath that made her breasts (high and firm, his mind reported happily, if uselessly) heave.

"Don't worry," he said. She had the look of a doe trapped in the headlights, which was ridiculous. What could he, mild-mannered physician and volleyball player, do to her, kick-ass princess? "I'm here to rescue you."

Her lips twitched at that and she sidled toward him, then dashed past him as he came forward to meet her, turning left out the door. He could hear her running lightly and damned quickly.

"Hey!" he yelled and took off after her. Blessed— or cursed—with a Texan-sized curiosity bump, he had to catch her. She could tell him why there had been a fight, who the unconscious man was, her name, and if she was free for dinner any night this week. This year. She was the most intriguing woman—certainly the most beautiful—he'd ever seen.

He couldn't say "he'd ever met" because they hadn't exactly been properly introduced. A fact he intended to remedy, posthaste. Part of him wondered what he was doing, chasing a stranger around hospital hallways in the wee hours of the morning. Another part of him urged him to run faster.

He caught sight of her just before she darted around a corner and forced himself to put on speed. *Come on, Dean, you wimp,* he thought contemptuously. *You've got to be a head taller at least— certainly your legs are longer. Catch up!* And, on the heels of that: *Where the hell is security? For that matter, where the hell is anybody?*

Speaking of dead ends, he just about had her cornered in one; she'd zigged when she should have zagged and there was no door at the end of this hallway, just a window, too far above her head to climb out. She was facing him, trapped with her back against the wall, when he jogged around the corner.

"There you are," he panted, slowing his pace. "Are you okay? Did that guy hurt you? Before you hurt him, I mean?"

Her eyes, which had been narrowed to blue slits studying him, now widened in surprise. He was hopelessly dazzled and gave in to the feeling—he was a long way between girlfriends and she really was spectacular. Had he thought her eyes were an ordinary blue? Coming closer, he could see they were the color of the sky on a cloudless day, pure and perfect. Paul Newman blue. Not that he was attracted to Paul. Because he wasn't. But the man had gorgeous eyes, and Jared was comfortable enough with his heterosexuality to admit it.

"If you're hurt," he said, trying not to wheeze, "I'd be glad to take a look at it for you. It's the least I can do, since you got me out of finishing my chart work. Dull stuff, believe me."

7

He heard himself babbling and told himself to shut up. She said nothing, just kept studying him. He noticed she wasn't even out of breath. *Kicking ass must keep her cardiovascular system in top form,* he thought.

"Seriously," he said. "*Are* you okay? Is there anything I can do? If you're in some kind of trouble, I can call a shelter, find you a safe place to stay."

Still she said nothing, but her lips twitched, as if fighting a smile. He wasn't sure what the joke was, but took a cautious step forward. "Everything's all right," he soothed, as if calming a wild doe, "now if I can just get you to come with me, I mean without rearranging my kidneys first, we'll find an exam room, make sure you're okay, and then we can talk about the trouble you're in. Whatever it is, I bet we can fix it if we put our heads together."

She opened her mouth and he waited eagerly, then they both heard the noise of pounding feet. *Well, well,* he thought tiredly, *what do you know—security finally woke up from ye olde one A.M. snoozefest.*

Whatever she had been about to say was forgotten as she reached up, just barely catching the bottom edge of the window. The hospital's windows were old—no wire mesh—and deep-set. He watched with utter astonishment as she grabbed hold of the ledge and flipped her legs up and over her head, her boots smashing through the glass and the rest of her following through.

He figured it was a good thing they were in the lowest level of the hospital, because he had the feeling she would have gone through that window

8

even if they'd been ten stories up. He wondered if the boots she wore had protected her from lacerations. Given the woman's incredible speed and luck, he assumed they had.

"Well, it was nice meeting you," he said numbly, and was nearly run over as two security guards came thundering around the corner. "She went thataway," he added, pointed to the shattered window. "And don't even try, she's long gone. Come on, I'll show you where the other one is."

The guards had a thousand questions. Jared couldn't tell them much and what he could tell them—the woman won, the woman was incredibly tough but seemed strangely vulnerable, the woman had eyes like the sky, the woman was going to be the mother of his children—he prudently kept to himself.

"You said the other one was in here, Dr. Dean?" one of the guards asked, and that was when Jared saw the woman's assailant was gone. The only thing left of him was a small puddle of blood on the table, presumably from a nosebleed. "Fan out," the guard said to the others, "he can't have gone far, not after Dr. Dean bashed him around."

"Actually," Jared began and then shut up. He didn't want to get the woman in more trouble, so he'd take the blame for KOing the bad guy. It hadn't been the first time people had taken in his size and assumed he was capable of violence. And he had been, in his youth—certainly he'd been in more of his share of after-school scuffles. But years of stitching up victims, of probing for bullets and setting smashed limbs, had made him lose his taste for it. "Uh . . . actually, I should get back to work."

"You got a description for us, doc?"

"For Nosebleed? Sure. About six-five, two hundred fifty pounds, shaved blond hair, one black eyebrow, one dislocated shoulder, one broken nose."

"Uh-huh," the guard asked, stepping close to Jared and sniffing him. This might have been intended to be a subtle move on the guard's part, except the man had a deviated septum and Jared could hear the shrill whistling intake when the man inhaled. "Broken nose, one eyebrow, we'll get right on it. You have anything to drink before you came on shift?" Sniff-sniff. Whistle-whistle.

"Don't be ridiculous," Jared snapped. "I gave up booze when I took up heroin. Seriously, I haven't had a drop. The bad guy really did look like some sort of mutated freak of nature. Now go get him!" *Before he catches up with what's-her-name,* he added silently.

The guards went, save for one who stayed behind to make sure Jared did his part of the dreary paperwork. Jared obediently followed him to the security office to fill out a report.

For the rest of his shift, he couldn't help looking over his shoulder and peeking around corners, as if the woman might have come back. Ridiculous thought . . . but Jared kept an eye out, regardless.

He wondered who she was.

# DOING IT RIGHT

\* \* \*

It took Kara an hour to stop trembling. Every time she started to calm down, the thought... *Jesus! He almost had me!*... would cycle back into her brain and she'd get the shakes again.

Carlotti, who'd been an utter creep since he was ten—and possibly before that—had chased her around like a dog, cornered her, and likely would have killed her—after having a little fun first, the raping swine—if she hadn't gotten the drop on him.

She had spotted him before she was even all the way through the door of the club and immediately turned and walked out. She started running when she heard him scrambling behind her and the chase was on.

Now, in the privacy of her apartment, she collapsed on her thirty-dollar thrift shop couch—tastefully upholstered in puke orange—and relived the chase. Carlotti was big but fast—and driven. If fear had been the fuel for her legs, hatred was his.

*Screw up one lousy drug shipment for the guy by siccing the Man on him,* she thought morosely, *and that was five years ago! And he's still holding a grudge, still wants to kill me. Guy's watched a few too many* God-father *movies.*

That was Carlotti's problem—one of his problems, anyway. He fancied himself a Corleone, when in reality he was a Clouseau. Everyone on the wrong side of the law knew the mob wasn't the all-seeing, vengeance-taking organization depicted

11

in the movies. And as for "organized crime"—ha! It wasn't organized at all. A few groups of loosely connected dealers, that was all. Sometimes they were successful in contracting crime to the local talent. Most times, not.

These days, the mob was a lot more interested in legitimate business—video arcades, karaoke bars, beauty salons. It was absolutely ridiculous how much a thriving salon could make in a fiscal year, especially if they also handled manicures. Lucrative and infinitely less dangerous than, say, running hookers.

Only the real idiots stayed in the drug trade, she knew. Too much heat, the feds had no tolerance for it, and the fall was long if you got pinched. Carlotti, of course, was a real idiot, and thus he fancied himself a mob drug lord. And, as a faithful disciple of mob movie fiction, he was still after her. As he'd proved tonight.

Shivering a little, she got up off the couch and headed for her mini bathroom. No shower, a cracked tub, and a rust-stained sink—the room was so small, when she sat on the toilet her knees touched the wall. It didn't matter. It was hers and she liked to think of it as a snug fox den, a haven from predators.

She sat down on the rim of the tub and started to fill it with warm water—after tonight, she needed to get Carlotti's stink off her—and thought about the idiot. She'd run for the hospital, naively thinking he wouldn't follow her to a well-lit, populated building. She hadn't counted on how deserted a hospital would be at three A.M. He'd finally cornered her and found out that a thief was never more dangerous than when her back was to the wall.

And the doctor who had seen everything—what was *that* about? He'd watched her, tried to warn her, and she could still feel the heat of his dark gaze. If she closed her eyes she could still see him—so broad-shouldered he nearly filled the doorway, with a lush mop of dark hair and the blackest eyes, strong, long-fingered hands, and a grin like lightning, a grin that lit up his whole face.

He'd chased her, but, to her surprise, not to hurt her or turn her in. To ask if she was all right. To ask if she needed a safe place to stay. She must have stared at him for an hour, or so it seemed. Who knows what she might have said—or done—if security hadn't shown up. His gaze had been so curiously intense and his smile, this marvelous charming smile . . .

A sudden thought made her straighten up so quickly she nearly tumbled into the tub. The doctor had seen Carlotti. And could testify against him. If the D.A. found out, he'd subpoena the doc in a nanosecond. The doc couldn't testify to much of anything, but anything was a start—didn't Capone go down for tax evasion? The D.A. would be glad to get Carlotti on trespassing and attempted assault, if only so that he could introduce his suspicions to a judge.

If word got out that there was one eyewitness, others would certainly follow . . . the D.A. could

13

build a case from whispers. God knew they did it all the time. And Carlotti's worst fear was doing time. When he was thirteen, he'd killed a witness to his shoplifting, just to avoid being shipped back to juvie.

The doctor was in very real danger. Carlotti had to shut him up, the sooner the better. The psycho wouldn't have to worry about her—the D.A. was at least as interested in putting her behind bars as he was in Carlotti—but he had to worry about the doctor. He probably had thugs working on the problem already.

"Crap," she sighed, and got up to make the first of several cups of coffee.

# Chapter 2

The next night, Jared was still thinking about the woman and still mentally yelling at himself to forget about her. *You'll never see her again,* he told himself, followed by, *Also, the whole thing was probably a hallucination brought on by too much paperwork. Proof that spending too much time on chart work is bad for you.* Trouble was, he couldn't get her out of his mind. Even now, when he was supposed to be snoozing in the third-floor on-call room, he was tossing and turning on the narrow, smelly bunk, fantasizing about what's-her-name instead of getting the sleep he needed. And the first rule of internship and residency was to sleep whenever you could. Sleep standing up if you had to.

He'd asked around, but no one knew of a beautiful blond goddess who ran like a deer and punched like a middleweight champion. Some of the nurses had suggested it was time he started dating again. One of the orderlies told him once he got more sleep, the hallucinations would stop. That was the trouble with being the hospital wiseass . . . when you had a serious problem, no one believed it.

*Tap-tap.*

Hell, it wasn't like he was hard up for female companionship. He worked with at least ten female docs and three times that many nurses. Not to mention X-ray techs, the lab ladies, the social workers—heck, wasn't the hospital chaplain a woman? One of the benefits of being an ER doc was that he got to visit all the wards, got to meet all the—

*Tap-tap.*

—staff outside his department and he should just—

*Tap-tap-tap.*

"What the hell *is* that?" he muttered, getting up and crossing the room. He had a flashback to one of his literature classes. "Who is that tapping, tapping at my chamber door?" he boomed, pulling back the curtain and expecting to see . . . he wasn't sure. A branch, rasping across the glass? A pigeon? Instead, he found himself gazing into a face ten inches from his own. "Aaiiggh!"

It was her. Crouched on the ledge, perfectly balanced on the balls of her feet, she had one small fist raised, doubtless ready to knock again. When she saw him, she gestured patiently to the lock. He dimly noticed she was dressed like a normal person instead of a burglar—navy leggings and a matching turtleneck—and wondered why she wasn't shivering with cold.

He groped for the latch, dry-mouthed with fear for her. They were three stories up! If she should lose her balance . . . if a gust of wind should come up . . . The latch finally yielded to his fumbling fingers and he wrenched the window open, grabbing for her. She leaned back, out of the reach of his arms, and his heart stopped—actually stopped, ka-THUD!—in his chest. He backpedaled away from the window. "Okay, okay, sorry, didn't mean to startle you, now would you please get your ass in here?"

She raised her eyebrows at him and complied, swinging one leg over the ledge and stepping down into the room as lightly as a ballerina. He collapsed on the cot, clutching his chest. "Could you please not ever *ever* do that again?" he gasped. "Christ! My heart! What's going on? How'd you get up there? Did the nurses lock all the entrances again? They do that when they're overworked—"

"'Quoth the Raven, nevermore'," she said, and helped herself to a cup of coffee from the pot set up next to the window. At his surprised gape, she smiled a little and tapped her ear. "Thin glass. I heard you through the window. 'While I pondered, nearly napping, suddenly there came a rapping, rapping at my chamber door.' I think that's how it goes. Poe was high most of the time, so it's hard to tell. Also, the man you saw me bludgeon into unconsciousness dropped a dime on you today."

"He what?"

"Dropped a dime. Rolled you over. Put you out. Phoned you in. Wants to clock you. Wants to drop

17

you. Made arrangements to have you killed, pronto. Sugar?"

"No thanks," he said numbly.

"I mean," she said patiently, "is there sugar?"

He pointed to the last locker on the left and thought to warn her too late. When she opened it (first wrapping her sleeve around her hand, he noticed, as she had with the coffee pot handle), several hundred tea bags, salt packets, and sugar cubes tumbled out, free of their overstuffed, poorly stacked boxes. She quickly stepped back, avoiding the rain of sweetener, then bent, picked a cube off the floor, blew on it, and dropped it into her cup. She shoved the locker door with her knee until it grudgingly shut, trapping a dozen or so tea bags and sugar packets in the bottom with a grinding sound that set his teeth on edge.

She went to the door, thumbed the lock with her sleeve, then came back and sat down at the rickety table opposite the cot. She took a tentative sip of her coffee and then another, not so tentative. He was impressed—the hospital coffee tasted like primeval mud, as it boiled and reboiled all day and night. "So that's the scoop," she said casually.

"You're here to kill me?" he asked, trying to keep up with the twists and turns of the last forty seconds. "You're the hitman? Hitperson?" *Who knocked for entry?* he added silently.

"Me? Do wet work?" She threw her head back and pealed laughter at the ceiling. She had, he noticed admiringly, a great laugh. Her hair was plaited in a long blond braid that reached halfway down her back. He wondered what it would look like unbound and spread across his pillow. "Oh, that's very funny, Dr. Dean."

"Thanks, I've got a million of 'em." Pause. "How did you know my name?"

She smiled. It was a nice smile, warm, with no condescension. "It wasn't hard to find out."

"What's *your* name?" he asked boldly. He should have been nervous about the locked door, about the threat to his life. He wasn't. Instead, he was delighted at the chance to talk to her, after a day of thinking about her and wondering how she was— *who* she was.

"Kara."

"That's gorgeous," he informed her, "and I, of course, am not surprised. You're so pretty! And so deadly," he added with relish, "you're like one of those flowers that people can't resist picking and then—bam! Big-time rash."

"Thanks," she said. "I think." She blushed, which gave her high color and made her eyes bluer. He stared, besotted. He didn't think women blushed anymore. He didn't think women who beat up thugs blushed at all. He was very much afraid his mouth was hanging open, and he was unable to do a thing about it. "Dr. Dean—"

"Umm?"

"—I'm not sure you understand the seriousness of the situation."

"Long, tall, and ugly is out to get me," he said, sitting down opposite her. He shoved a pile of charts aside; several clattered to the floor and she watched them fall, amused. "But since you're not the hitman, I'm not too worried."

"Actually, I'm your self-appointed bodyguard."

"Oh, well, then I'm not worried at all," he said with feigned carelessness, while his brain chewed that one—*bodyguard?*—over.

"You could take on an assassin with one hand while writing a grocery list with the other. You're certainly a match for whoever that guy sends after me. So, do I pay you? Should we even be talking about money? What's the etiquette here?"

She blinked. "Uh . . . that won't be necessary. Dr. Dean—"

"Jared."

"—may I say, you're taking this remarkably well?"

"Work in an ER for a year," he said, suddenly grim. "You learn to recover your equilibrium pretty damned quickly."

"Touché," she said quietly.

"So now what?"

"Now you don't get killed."

"I mean, what happens now? What do we do?"

"We?"

"We've got to sic the cops on the bad guy, right? Do we, er, drop a dime on him?"

"No cops!" she yelped, startling him. She hadn't been this rattled when Uggo had been trying to smash her face in. "We'll keep you out of trouble until this blows over. End of plan."

"Blows over?" he practically shouted. "I have to—we have to put our lives on hold until ole One

Eyebrow goes away? Forgive me, but I thought you were a little more pro-active than that."

"You're right," she admitted, "but when the law is involved, I can't be as pro-active as I'd like."

"But . . . aren't you in trouble, too? Won't Jerk-off try to kill you?"

"Oh, he's been trying," she said casually, as if a large, frightening, ugly man trying to kill her was of as much consequence as a threatened spring shower. "For years. He'll never get me. Too dumb. Too slow."

"Too lame a bad guy, sounds like," he muttered. "It's almost embarrassing to be on his shit list."

She frowned. "This is serious. You're a sitting duck because you're different."

"You mean because I have two eyebrows?"

She giggled into her cup and he was absurdly pleased with himself. "I mean, you're a citizen. A taxpayer, one of the good guys. Not like Carlotti."

He pounced. "Not like you?"

The smile vanished, *poof!* "You ask a lot of questions, Dr. Dean."

"Jared. And you're still in trouble with this guy, same as I am. Who's going to look out for you? I mean, if you get sick or short of breath or have chest pains, I'm your man, but if a hit squad starts shooting at you to shut you up, I'll be the one cowering in the corner with my hands over my ears."

She smiled and tried to hide it, but he saw it and grinned back at her. "Carlotti knows he has nothing to fear from me in court," she explained, getting up to refill her cup. She disdained the sugar locker and drank it black, making an appreciative face. He couldn't believe it—of all the things to happen this evening, beautiful Kara enjoying the hospital's interpretation of coffee was the strangest. "I can't testify against him."

She didn't elaborate, but Jared was able to figure that one out. There were only two reasons not to testify against anyone: fear—which Kara didn't seem to know the meaning of—and having something to hide. You didn't testify for the D.A. if the D.A. had something on you as well.

He wondered what she had done.

"So let's go see the D.A.," he said, seizing the bull by the horns.

"You may, if you like," she said quietly, "but you'll go alone and I would prefer to wait and see what happens."

Which meant she knew a lot more than she was telling. He had the feeling that if he insisted on seeing the D.A., he'd for a fact never see her again.

He instantly decided that was an unacceptable course of action. Screw the risk to his personal health! He had to get to know this woman.

"So . . . what?"

"We wait until Carlotti is arrested. It shouldn't be long. A lot of people are looking for him." She said that with cool relish and he made a mental note to never get on her bad side. "When he's arrested, you're out of danger."

"Doesn't he have hench-thugs who could still get me?"

She nodded. "In theory. But they won't make a move without him breathing in their ears. You can see the D.A.—his name is Thomas Wechter, by the way, second floor of the courthouse, take a left past the water fountain—and tell him your story, tell him you're willing to testify, ask to see the rest of his case. If he has one."

"What about you?" he asked, trying once again, even though he knew it was useless. The same tenacity that made other doctors literally pull him off a DOA wouldn't let him back away from this. "You were wronged by Carstupidi. You should testify that he tried to kill you! I mean, Jesus, that big bully, if you hadn't cleaned his clock, I would have."

She snorted and he raised an eyebrow at her. "Sorry," she said quickly. "I was just picturing you and Carlotti—but you were talking about the D.A. I can't testify. It's all up to you."

"What are you afraid of?" he asked boldly, sure she'd rebuff him, or deny fear. Instead, she just gave him a level look.

"Nothing I could explain to you," she said quietly, then got up, poured the rest of her coffee down the sink and walked to the window. She took the cup with her, he noticed. After a moment, he got it—she was so paranoid, she wouldn't take a chance on leaving fingerprints behind. Interesting. "See you around, Dr. Dean. I'll be in touch." She stepped up to the windowsill.

*"It's Jared,"* he yelled, darting after her, "and use the *door,* for God's sake! Look, it's right here." He

rattled the doorknob invitingly; she ignored him. "I can walk you to the main entrance. Ha! Some bodyguard!" he screamed and that got her attention; she paused and turned, looking at him over her shoulder, one foot already on the ledge. "Leaving me here to rot! I'm easy pickings for Carlotti's hench-morons."

She smiled. "Hardly. I'll be close. Good night."

"Wait!" But the window closed firmly and when he darted to it to look out, it was so dark he couldn't see her anymore.

Ten hours later, he let himself into his apartment. A long shift, but a busy and rewarding one—only one death and that one a DNR, an eighty-seven-year-old woman who had been praying for death for the better part of a year, according to her calmly tearful daughter. Tough, but it could have been so much worse. Was so much worse, frequently.

He often wondered how he had ended up where he was—a physician, someone who dealt with death every day. In school he'd been an amiable goof-off, the class clown, never taking anything or anyone seriously. Strange that he had been drawn to a career that was, at times, absolutely the furthest thing from humorous.

It wasn't that he'd lost someone close to him, had been marked forever by the death of a parent or close friend. Hell, he'd never had so much as a pet die on him. But in college he'd taken an EMT course, and as part of the training he had to volunteer at a busy metro hospital.

Looking at the suffering around him, he watched the doctors and nurses ease that suffering, pull off miracle cures, reunite families. He remembered thinking, *That looks a helluva lot more satisfying than working in an office or going out to L.A. to do stand-up. Making people laugh is one thing. Giving them their lives back is another.* He had gone home that night and applied to five premed programs. His father, seeing his slack-ass son filling out college applications instead of watching *Friends* reruns, had nearly wept with relief.

He was walking through the living room, intent on the kitchen and a sandwich, when he saw Kara was deeply asleep on his couch, curled under a yellow fleece throw. He nearly walked into the end table.

He turned around, tiptoed back to his front door, and examined the lock. Absolutely no signs of tampering. Then he walked to the windows, which were all locked on the inside. The woman was a marvel, a ghost—a rich woman if she ever decided to use her powers to aid the forces of evil.

He went to stand over her again, wanting to talk to her, but also wanting to let her sleep. If she had stayed close, as she said she would—and he didn't think she would lie to him—she'd had a long day, most of it probably spent huddled on ledges. She hadn't heard him come in through the door and he hadn't been taking particular care to be quiet. Clearly she was exhausted. He would let her sleep.

Except . . .

Except her hair, in the faint gleam from the streetlight, was muted gold, the color of nuggets brought up from the river, gleaming dully among the pebbles and worth thousands. It was the first time he'd seen it down and he itched to touch, caress . . .

He reached out a trembling hand and stroked her hair where it curved along her skull, realizing with happy dismay that he was falling in love with a woman he knew nothing about, not even her last name.

It was his last happy thought for a while. She came awake like a cat in the dark—one minute dead to the world, the next utterly alert. Her hand came up, seized his wrist in a grip slightly less breakable than handcuffs, and pulled. Hard. He rocketed toward her and somehow—he didn't think this was possible to do from a prone position—she flipped him over the end of the couch. She didn't let go of his wrist and a split second later he was on his butt in the dust and she was looking down at him from the back of the couch, still holding his wrist, which started to throb from the pressure.

"For heaven's sake," she complained, letting go. "Don't scare me like that."

He could feel his eyes bulge. "Don't *scare* you?" he croaked, climbing slowly to his feet. "You're the one who broke in, dammit! Jesus Christ, I come into my apartment—*my* apartment—and here you are, dead to the world, a—a breaker and enterer—"

"I didn't break," she said reasonably. "Just entered."

"—and then you wake up and kick my ass all over my own living room. Who scared who?" He finished standing and was pleasantly surprised to find his legs were supporting him. His heart rate felt quite high—like about six hundred. "Some bodyguard!"

She snorted, then the snort turned into a laugh. She choked off the sound almost at once and looked at him, stone-faced. "I apologize for startling you. Something woke me up—"

He coughed, knowing his pawing her hair had been what awakened her and unwilling to impart that information at the moment.

"—and then I saw a large man—"

"A large, incredibly handsome, virile man," he interrupted.

"—leaning over me and I acted instinctively. How's the wrist? Good thing I didn't break it on the way down," she added thoughtfully.

"Yes, that *is* a good thing. I retract my whining. Instead I'll count my blessings. You could have broken my arm, caved in my skull, reached into my chest, and pulled out my still beating heart and showed it to me."

She looked away. "I'm not quite that bad. You have—" she eyed him as he hustled toward the kitchen, remembering he hadn't eaten in seven hours—"admirable equilibrium."

"That's what all my bodyguards say," he replied

affably over his shoulder. "How about some break-fast?"

"That would be lovely," she admitted, carefully folding the blanket she had been using. She placed it gently at the end of the couch and followed him into the kitchen. "I hope you don't mind my coming here. I didn't hurt your lock—"

"I don't mind," he assured her. "You can come over anytime. Do you want a key?"

"It's not necessary," she said with a straight face.

"I *know* that. But maybe it'll be a little faster than picking my lock every . . . No?" She shook her head. "Ho, boy. That's some childhood you must have had."

She changed the subject—but later, when he thought about the conversation, he realized she hadn't changed it at all. "How is the little boy?"

He looked up from removing ingredients from the refrigerator. "Little boy?"

She perched on a stool beside the counter. "He came in the ER with multiple stab wounds. Red hair, about seven years old?"

"Ah. He was stable when I left. Amazingly, the bastard who did the cutting managed to miss virtually every major organ and blood vessel. His mother's boyfriend," Jared added, whipping eggs in a stainless steel bowl. "Carved the kid up when Mama left him. In Cleopatra's time, they used strangulation as the death penalty. Kind of makes you long for the good old days, huh?"

She nodded seriously, though he had—he

thought he had—been joking. Dark humor, the kind he took refuge in when terrible things happened to little kids. To anyone. "Someone *should* kill the boyfriend," she said matter-of-factly. "That kind never stops." She drummed her fingers on the counter, thinking.

"Now wait a minute," he protested. "I can see you trying to fit killing the boyfriend into your busy schedule—between bodyguarding me and grocery shopping and single-handedly cracking every safe on the block—and you've got to forget it. If you killed everybody you thought deserved it, you'd never be done."

"Don't you think someone who stabs a little boy five times deserves to be removed from the planet?"

"I think it's not our call."

She snorted, such an incongruous sound with her delicate exterior that he nearly laughed out loud. "Spoken like a true sheep."

He grated cheese irritably. "What, because I don't go around like Vince the Vigilante, I'm a sheep?"

"No," she said patiently, "you're a sheep because you don't right wrongs."

He slammed the bowl on the counter and leaned across it, until his face was two inches from hers. "I had that child's blood up to my elbows," he said evenly. "Don't tell me I don't right wrongs." He leaned back, forcing his temper down. "And how'd you know about the kid, anyway? I didn't see you in the ER all night."

"I apologize."

"Don't be sorry, just use the *door* once in a while so I can see you coming and going."

She didn't smile, just looked at him with serious eyes. "You know what I meant."

"Yes," he said, whittling away at a shallot until it was a delicate pile of white and purple shavings. "I know and I accept with thanks. For the record, I run into plenty of people whose lungs I'd like to remove without benefit of anesthesia. But if I concentrated on that, I couldn't do my job. Saving lives is more important to me than avenging them."

She shifted on her stool, causing the white T-shirt she wore to mold to her breasts for a moment. He looked away before he accidentally cut off his thumb. "That sounds nice. You're great at your job, I could tell. The nurses," she added dryly, "seem especially impressed with your . . . hands."

He waved the knife at her. "Go on," he said modestly.

"It's true."

"I said go on. Do they talk about how tall I am, how handsome, how smart, how I'm the most fascinating man they've ever known, the finest doctor, the best volleyball player?"

"They talk about how it's been a while since you were caught in the meds closet with one of the orthopedic surgeons."

He winced. "One time! It was only one time. I was young."

"It was last year."

"I've grown decades since then in wisdom. What else do you want in your omelet?"

"Whatever you're having. Don't change the subject. Are you still seeing her?"

"God, no." He poured two large glasses of milk. "She used me to get even with her fiancé. A ten-minute grope in the closet and she was off to confess her infidelity and demand he start paying attention to her, uh, needs."

"Ouch."

"Tell me," he said gloomily, sliding the raw egg mixture into the pan. "And somehow I ended up with this ridiculous stud reputation. Most of the women who come on to me are looking for a no-commitment quickie and the ones I'd like to get to know think I'm a pig and won't have anything to do with me."

"That's too bad," she said, and he jerked his head up at her tone. She hadn't sounded sympathetic. She'd sounded almost . . . pleased?

"It's what I deserve," he sighed, "for giving in to her womanly wiles."

"What about your wiles? More milk, please," she added when he opened the fridge to put the carton away.

"I am wile-less. And you never answered my question—how'd you know about the boy? And the orthopedic surgeon, for that matter," he added under his breath.

"It's an inner-city emergency room," she pointed out, looking on with interest as he slid a perfect omelet onto her plate. "I could walk in on my hands and the only one to notice would be the triage nurse and the only thing *she'd* want to know was my insurance number."

"Can you?" he asked, beginning to cook his own omelet.

"What?" she asked with her mouth full.

"Walk on your hands?"

She swallowed, dabbed her lips—full and pouty, his mind reported uselessly—grinned at him, then arched backward on her stool. In a moment her head and torso had disappeared and he could see her legs receding as she carefully walked away from him on her hands.

He applauded. She came back to her feet, slightly flushed and looking pleased, and took her seat, rubbing her hands on her thighs. "You're amazing," he said admiringly. "You can do everything."

"You wouldn't like me if you really knew me," she said, then pressed her lips together so hard they went white. He had the feeling she wasn't in the habit of making candid comments to near strangers.

"What's not to like?" he said, trying to sound casual, to cover up the bald truth in his question.

She shook her head at him and finished her omelet in silence. "Wonderful," she said, pushing the empty plate away. "The best breakfast I ever had. Where did you learn to cook?"

"My dad was a chef."

"Was?"

"He and my mom retired and moved to North Carolina. Now they golf and wear ugly clothes and make fun of the tourists. It's a shameful thing, I've been searching for a cure for them. Where are your folks?" He rinsed the plates in silence, sure she wouldn't answer him.

"Dead," she said finally. "They died when I was just a kid. I went to a foster family the week after they died, and when my foster mother broke my arm I ran away."

"Jesus." He crossed the room, wanting to take her into his arms, not sure how to bridge the sudden gulf between them. "That's terrible."

"It's no big deal," she said quickly. "It's not like I remember my parents. You don't miss what you never had."

"Wrong, gorgeous. That's the stuff you miss most of all." And carefully, so carefully, he put his arms around her and drew her close.

"You don't know what you're talking about," she said, staring at his mouth.

"Want to bet?"

Her mouth was a dream, the nicest dream he'd ever had, all sweet lips and lush softness. She pressed against him and he felt her breasts flatten slightly against his chest, felt her arms come around him, felt her mouth bloom beneath his. She sighed into his mouth and he shuddered, balling his hands into fists so he wouldn't tear off her clothes and take her on the kitchen tile, which hadn't been mopped since he was a med student. He heard her make a sound, some sound, a cross

33

between a growl and a whimper, and heard himself groan in response. Then she came to herself—or perhaps came away from herself, back to the cool exterior she liked to show the world—and stiffened, took her arms away and pushed him back.

"I'm sorry," he said, not very, but not interested in gaining a black eye either, "but you're so beautiful and—and good, I can't resist you."

She looked startled, then sad. "I'm not good. I'm bad. You should keep it in mind, Jared." She touched her mouth, then looked at him with something like wonder.

"Anybody who has Carlotti for an enemy—who would protect a stranger from her enemy—isn't bad."

"I've done . . . terrible things. You wouldn't understand."

"Try me," he urged softly. He took a step toward her and she skittered back, nearly tripping over the stool to keep away from him. He was struck once again by the combination of power and vulnerability. She could snap his spine like a breadstick, he was sure. And yet, she was afraid of his touch. "Or not," he joked, hoping to lighten the mood. "Hey, I've done terrible things, too. In med school one time, I brought my cadaver to breakfast at the local Denny's. Man," he said nostalgically, "the food inspector sure got pissed. On the bright side, my cadaver was a cheap date."

She giggled, then choked off the sound and looked at him severely. "No more of that," she said.

"I'm here to keep you safe for a few days, not to play wifey."

"Don't *play* wifey," he said promptly, "marry me."

"Ha, ha."

He decided not to mention the fact that he wasn't kidding. "So now what happens?" he asked.

# Chapter 3

Good question, Kara thought, once again stretched out on the couch. She had decided to look after Dr. Dean—*Jared*—for a very simple reason and her conscience had nothing to do with it. He had chased her not to hurt her or turn her in, but to ask if she was all right. That was when she realized Carlotti would come after him. That was why she was here.

Jared's stunning good looks, great sense of humor, and outstanding dedication to helping others had nothing to do with it. There were plenty of good-looking men in the world. Gorgeous, dark-haired men with lightning smiles. With a sense of common decency that was as much a part of him as his white coat and stethoscope. Phenomenal at healing and cooking, stitching head gashes with the same hands that whipped up a perfectly fluffy omelet. Dr. Dean was nothing special. Not him.

That surgeon, she thought with disgust. The bimbo

who used him and dumped him. He was too good for someone that idiotic.

She slammed the pillow over her head, muffling a groan. *And if he's too good for a surgeon,* she reminded herself savagely, *he's a damn sight too good for you, silly bitch.*

So the question remained—now what happened?

Sleep. Then lunch. He hadn't wanted to go to bed; he'd wanted to keep talking to her. She first thought it might have been because he was interested in knowing her as a person, but that was too conceited to be considered for more than a moment. No, she was interesting to him, like a virus was interesting, if dangerous. He knew she could shake up his nice little life and so he was drawn to her, the way the new kids at juvie were drawn to the ones who graduated to robbery and murder.

So he'd kept after her, talking to her and asking questions and telling her about himself, and when she reminded him he hadn't slept in twenty hours, he had looked stubborn and shrugged and asked her what her earliest memory was, because his was of his dad chopping onions while onion-tears streamed down his face and ever since then he'd felt kind of funny about onions, they were "the meanest vegetable." Tomatoes were the nicest, so round and sweet and juicy, they were—

She interrupted him, he argued, they bargained. He agreed to sleep for a few hours if she would let him take her to lunch when he woke. To which she agreed, looking forward to the lunch and mad at herself for looking forward to it.

He had given her a longing look over his shoulder as he trudged to his solitary bed, and she'd been ridiculously tempted to follow him and undress him and find out if he was as good at other things as he was at kissing.

But that was madness, pure and simple, and she wasn't about to open herself up to a citizen, someone who didn't know the first thing about survival or what she had been through. Someone who would be shocked and horrified at what she did. Someone who would wait around long enough for her to love him, then abandon her once she depended on him.

Dr. Jared Dean was the best kisser in the world. And she didn't intend to find out anything beyond that.

It was no use. He couldn't sleep. He pulled his pillow from beneath his head and punched it. It was too hot—*he* was too hot—and Kara was too close.

The more he tried to ignore the fact that The Delectable One was sleeping just a few feet away, the randier he got. It wasn't fair. Why couldn't his bodyguard be dull and ugly? Uncomplicated and bow-legged?

*It's just because you're in a dry spell,* he told himself. *When was the last time you got horizontal with anybody? The last time you got some nooky, they were still debating whether Gore or Bush had won the election. Right? So just . . . put her out of your mind.*

Right. Sure. Piece of cake. Ha!

As if in response to his frustration, his door creaked open with ominous slowness. Jared clutched the blanket beneath his chin and stared at the large, menacing silhouette framed in the doorway. He was a fan of horror movies, so he knew he was about to be stalked, chased, then cut in half with a table saw, only to be saved at the last minute so he could appear in the sequel. A *bad* sequel.

"Leave me alone," he said to the approaching silhouette. "Go find Jennifer Love Hewitt."

The silhouette stopped short of his bed. His curtains were wide open, and as the moon came out from behind the clouds he saw it was Kara. Her silhouette was menacingly huge because she was wearing an armadillo suit.

"That's a new look for you," he observed.

"God, I want you," she replied, approaching so quickly her armadillo tail knocked everything off his bedside table. "You're all I can think about, Jared."

"That's nice. Really! Uh, what are you doing?"

She was unscrewing the jar she was holding. Then she tossed the lid behind her where it hit the floor with a clatter. She reached into the jar with her armadillo paw and extracted something small and wet. Which she flung at him.

Jared felt the pickle slice hit his forehead with a wet smack. "Pickled vegetables make me *sooooo* horny," she whispered. She then upended the jar all over herself. Pickle juice rained down on his floor—and her armadillo suit. She writhed and moaned within the dill-scented shower.

"On any other day, I would find this extremely weird." In fact, he felt pretty sanguine about what was happening. "However, it's been one of those days, so nothing surprises me."

He heard a purring sound as she unzipped her armadillo suit and stepped out of it. For a moment she was naked in the moonlight, her skin almost alabaster in the eerie light. Then she pounced on him. Her breasts brushed his chin as she leaned forward and sucked the pickle off his forehead. He heard her crunch, gulp, then felt her tongue as it slid back and forth across his forehead.

"Ummmm," she moaned, "Vlassic."

"Uh . . . Kara . . . are you on any medication that you think I should—"

"Shut up and take me," she commanded, her breath redolent with dill. "Take me like you know I want to be taken."

"Okay . . . but I'll have to stop and fill up my gas tank first."

"Stop that. There's something you should know."

"I can't imagine what the hell it could be," he said with perfect truth.

"When I eat pickles . . . afterwards, I must always wash them down with cock."

"Wha—aigh!" Shockingly, she reached back and grabbed him. Even more shocking, he was as firm as a crisp pickle.

Quick as a fish, she whipped around and dived

for his dick like a gull diving for a herring. Instantly her warm, wet mouth was on him, while he was face-to-face, so to speak, with her delectable ass. It looked good enough to eat. He leaned forward and gently bit down on the plump, smooth flesh.

She hummed in response, which sent glorious vibrations through his dick, vibrations he felt all the way up to his eyeballs.

Her head was pistoning up and down like that stupid woodpecker toy he had as a kid. And speaking of peckers, his was so hard he felt like it had to be three feet long. Her lips surrounded him, her teeth scraped him—very, very gently—and he groaned around a mouthful of her ass.

There was a *pop* as she pulled her mouth free of him. Then she whipped back around, straddling him. She laced her fingers behind his neck and jerked him into a sitting position. "I want you," she growled, sounding uncommonly like the kid from *The Exorcist*. She smelled strongly of pickles. Her breasts pressed against his chest.

"That's swell," he said, "because I want you, too, but maybe we could slow down a little—"

"Less talk," she murmured. "More fucking."

"Okey dokey."

She seized him, accidentally catching several pubic hairs. He let out a yelp, but by then she was stuffing him inside her. She rode him enthusiastically, squealing happily every time she impaled herself. Her breasts bobbed. Pickle juice dripped from her shoulders. He held onto the side of the bed for dear life as his orgasm thundered closer, closer . . .

She twisted, jerked, bounced. He started to come at the exact moment her momentum pushed him from the bed. He slammed into the—

Floor.

Jared jerked awake, staring at the ceiling. The armadillo suit was gone. So was the lingering odor of pickles and, of course, Kara. He had semen on his stomach and one fuck of a headache.

"Jesus Christ," he gasped, then started the long climb back into bed.

The thump of Jared flailing his way off the bed inserted itself into Kara's dream as his bedroom door slammed open.

She sat up on the couch and saw him walking softly toward her, splendidly naked. His shoulders were broad and his chest was lightly furred with crisp black hair, hair that tapered down past his belly button into his lush pubic hair. His sex jutted toward her. He wasn't smiling.

She saw, with no real surprise, that she was naked, too.

"Come closer," he said, even as he did so himself, and then he was standing before her, his hand on the back of her neck, urging her forward. "Touch me."

"I—"

"With your mouth, Kara. Touch me with your mouth. I want you to, and *you* want you to."

"It's a secret." The wanting. The craving.

"I won't tell." The pressure on the back of her neck increased, and she opened her lips and took him. His long, rolling purr of satisfaction kindled her own excitement.

His palms were on either side of her face as he rocked his hips against her mouth. Then he pulled away and knelt between her legs. He spread her thighs wide and pushed her back, then pulled her legs across his. His hands were busy at the small of her back, pulling her toward him, and she felt him enter her with sweet and delicious slowness.

She tried to bring her arms around him but, strangely, couldn't move them an inch. She was pushed back so far, her legs were so wide. He crouched and rode her, rode her. It was hard to get a breath. It was hard to even want to.

"When I'm done," he said, perfectly calm, "I'll leave."

"Yes, that's—"

"—what people do, yes. I know. You didn't think you could have a normal life with me, did you?"

"Why can't I?"

"Why *should* you?" He pulled out and, with savage swiftness, flipped her over. Shoved her, hard. She grabbed wildly for the couch, and found herself bent over the arm rest. Felt him part her legs, and brutally shove himself inside her. Red agony slashed across her vision as he shoved and withdrew and pushed some more. His fingers dug into her flesh, marking it, and she squirmed to get away.

To her extreme humiliation, beneath the pain she could sense something else begin to stir.

"Say it."

She said nothing. He shoved, harder than he ever had, so hard she could almost feel his cock in the back of her throat. His fingers were busy between her legs, pinching the tender lips, pulling on them. He withdrew almost all the way and she went limp, thinking he was done, and then he rammed himself into her again. She made a sound between a moan and a scream.

"Say it or I'll stop."

Everything was tightening, was getting hotter, and it hurt, God, it hurt, but it felt embarrassingly marvelous, too, and he couldn't stop before she found her climax, he couldn't. "Everybody leaves."

"Good. Yes. Everybody leaves." Although his brutal thrusting didn't stop, his fingers between her thighs became gentle, toyed with her throbbing clit, swept over it, squeezed it, rubbed, rubbed, rubbed . . .

Things went dark, very dark around the edges as her orgasm screamed through her. She lay across the armrest for a moment, gasping, then turned over.

He was gone.

The next day, Jared and Kara managed to get up, refresh themselves, have a pleasant conversation, and leave together without actually making eye contact.

Jared crept around the apartment feeling guilty, and nearly screamed when he opened the fridge and saw the jar of pickles sitting menacingly on the second shelf.

For her part, Kara was mortified. She prayed Jared couldn't read her expression. She didn't like pain, she had *never* liked pain, she certainly didn't like anybody messing with her ass, so what was with that dream? In real life, if Jared ever tried such a thing, she'd break his arm in two places.

Right?

After driving downtown to find a restaurant, they'd parked the car and walked, enjoying the unseasonably warm weather. Indian summer had been going on for more than a month. *Chicago in October,* Kara mused. *You gotta love it.*

Jared stopped in his tracks so suddenly, she went two steps past him before realizing he wasn't walking. "You want to eat here?"

Surprised, Kara turned to look at him. "You said I could choose. If you don't like sushi, they have other things. You can have a steak or—"

"It's not that."

The man looked decidedly nervous; she wondered what was up. Jared seemed singularly unconcerned about his life being in danger, but ill at ease when confronted with the prospect of a Japanese restaurant.

"What's wrong?"

He was looking through the front window, shading his eyes and squinting. "It's okay," he said at last. "I don't think he's working right now. We can go in."

He pulled open the door to Ish, a trendy sushi restaurant with a terrible name and astonishing food. He held the door for her and, with a wary look inside, she went in. The interior, like every Japanese restaurant she had ever been in, was understated and completely different from the outside. The building housing the restaurant was gray cement, the entrance to the restaurant shaded with a dirty green awning. Inside, however, the carpet was pearl gray and immaculate, plain ink prints decorated the walls, the tables were low, and the wood had been rubbed to a mellow glow. Muted music tinkled over the speakers, waitresses wearing beautiful kimonos shuffled quietly to and fro, and the air smelled of soup and delicate Japanese spices.

Kara took an appreciative breath while they waited for a table. She loved the way the Japanese did things, their understated efficiency, the beauty of their food presentation, their droll humor. She adored the cuisine and could have eaten sushi three times daily. Too bad Jared looked ready to jump out of his skin. She could sense no danger to him here, but resolved to keep her eyes open.

The hostess stepped toward them, dressed in a sapphire blue kimono embroidered with white seagull silhouettes. She bowed a greeting, then asked them pleasantly if they wanted smoking or non.

"Non," they said in unison, then followed her to a table by the window.

"Excuse me," Kara said, "but we'd prefer a table at the back of the room, if you please."

The hostess apologized and led them to a booth in the back. When she was gone, while they were wiping their faces with the hot, damp towels she had left them, Jared said, "You don't want me sitting by the window, huh?"

Kara shrugged. "Force of habit. Listen, you're making me nervous. What's the problem? Why don't you like this place?"

"I love this place," he assured her. "The food is fabulous, the service is great."

"Then why—"

"It's a long story. Never mind. What are you having?"

Before she could answer, a voice boomed, "Ah, Dr. Dean!" Jared sighed.

"Busted," he muttered, just before a middle-aged Japanese man rushed to their table. The man was wiry and looked strong. His head was so bald and shiny Kara itched to touch it, to see if it felt as smooth as it looked.

"Hello, hello! So nice to see you again and you've brought a lovely lady friend, too, how wonderful!"

"Ishiguro, this is Kara. Kara, this is the owner, Ishiguro. Listen, pal," Jared said to the beaming man, "let's not do this, okay?"

Kara edged closer to the edge of the booth, ready

to pound the man into jelly if he so much as twitched a trigger finger. Jared promptly stuck his foot up onto her seat, barring her way.

Ishiguro quit smiling and looked stubborn. He snapped his fingers and a waitress appeared, bowing to him and then to Jared and Kara. "These are my dear good friends," he said, "and they must have anything they want. Bring appetizers. Dr. Dean is partial to seafood."

The waitress bowed again and practically sprinted to the kitchen.

"Ishiguro," Jared said warningly.

The man rapped something sharp in Japanese and Jared shut up. Ishiguro turned to Kara and said, "Do you know the story of how the wonderful Dr. Dean saved my only son from hideous death?"

"He probably would have been able to cough it up on his own," Jared mumbled.

"Please tell me," Kara said politely.

"It's not that big a deal," Jared protested.

Ishiguro ignored him. "There he was, my poor Yoshi, gagging and turning blue and staggering, and we pounded on his back and prayed an ambulance would come, when Dr. Dean leaped from his chair, over the table—"

"I did *not*."

"—and with a squeeze of his mighty arms—"

"For God's sake."

"—forced the offending fish from my son's throat. Ah! He breathed, he lived, he is first in his class at Harvard Business, he is married and his

49

lovely wife is pregnant with my first grandchild."
Ishiguro stopped and looked at Jared admiringly.
"All because of Dr. Dean. So."

Kara looked at Jared. "I'm betting lunch is on
the house."

Jared nodded unhappily. "Come on, Ish, you've
given me enough free meals, you've probably cost
yourself a thousand bucks in food. I was glad to
help, but I was only doing my job, you don't need
to keep giving me—"

Ishiguro held up a hand imperiously. When he
spoke, his voice was very mild, but his gaze was arc-
tic. "Are you suggesting my son's life is not worth
some raw fish and rice?"

"Uh, no."

"Are you suggesting there is no debt between
us?"

Jared sighed. Kara smiled. "Give it up, Jared. Besides, you're insulting our host."

"The lady is wise," Ishiguro declared, just as the
waitress reappeared, carrying a large tray crowded
with enticing dishes.

Ishiguro placed the food himself, clucking over
them like a hen with two chicks, making sure the
temperature of the food was exactly right, Kara
waited for him to tie a napkin around Jared's neck
and start hand-feeding him, but he didn't go that
far. And then, finally, he left them to their food.

Kara had to laugh. Poor Jared looked so embarrassed, she almost felt sorry for him. "No wonder
you didn't want to come in here," she said, digging

into her *chawanmushi,* a delicately flavored custard crammed with seafood and mushrooms.

"It's not just the fuss he makes," Jared confessed in a low voice. "I swear, he loses money every time I come in. Then I avoid the place for a few months and his feelings are hurt . . . It's kind of a mess."

"That will teach you to save lives, you bastard," she said solemnly and they both laughed.

They had barely begun their meal when Jared's pager went off. He sighed, swallowed, and unclipped it for a quick glance. "I've got to go back to the hospital," he said. "Let me call you a cab."

"I'm coming with you," she said, tossing her napkin on the table.

"No, Kara, stay here and enjoy the food, you—"

"This isn't a date, Jared," she reminded him coolly, though she'd had trouble remembering that fact herself. "I'm sticking close for the next few days. Besides, it's not hard to get your pager number. For all you know, this is a trick. I'm coming with you."

He looked pleased. She had no idea why. "Okay. I'll call us both a cab." They stood, and, as Ishiguro approached, he waved his pager at the restaurant owner. "Gotta run, Ish. Everything was fabulous. I'm sorry we couldn't finish."

"That's quite all right, Dr. Dean. We'll box it up and send it to the hospital for a late snack. I hope you'll stop back later for dinner." He shook Jared's hand, then beamed with surprised delight when Kara bowed. She did it out of a perverse, continual

51

need to prove her late sensei, a man similar to Ishiguro in looks but quite dissimilar in temperament, wrong. He'd told her once, when she was very small, that Americans bowed like cows danced. She'd spent as much time trying to perfect her bow as she had trying to perfect her defensive techniques.

Ishiguro, smiling, returned her bow and they left.

At the hospital, she watched Jared work and was impressed all over again. He was deft, compassionate, constantly smiling, and if he felt it was appropriate, gently teasing. The patients seemed to adore him. Certainly the nurses were fond of him. She bristled as more than one nurse "accidentally" brushed by Jared, touched his arm, laughed a bit too loudly at his jokes. Then she scolded herself for bristling.

Calling Jared back to the hospital had not been a trick. Still, Kara kept a wary eye out. She hadn't heard any word on the street about Carlotti, which was good news, so far. Carlotti was like a freight train—slow to get going, almost unstoppable once he reached full speed. When things started to happen, they would happen fast. For now, she and Jared could enjoy the calm before the storm.

Hunger gnawed at her, but she ignored the sensation. It was too bad their lunch had been interrupted, but they could grab a bite or maybe chow on leftovers when Jared finished his work. She certainly wasn't planning to leave him alone while she stuffed her face.

She saw he was looking for her and stepped up behind him, tapping his shoulder. He turned and blinked with surprise when he saw it was her. "How do you do that?" he said, half complaining, half admiring. "I've been looking all over for you and I never see you unless you want me to."

"Inner city emergency room," she reminded him. "Remember?"

"Right. Don't walk on your hands to prove your point, I get it. And I'm *starving*. The interns grabbed our leftovers, the bastards. Want to get some supper?"

She glanced at the clock and saw with a start that she had been watching and admiring and thinking about him for close to five hours. It felt like five minutes.

She nodded and he reached for her hand, unthinking. She stiffened for a moment, then let him hold her hand. His fingers were warm and—odd!—she felt their warmth all the way down to her toes. "I'm sorry you had to wait so long," he was saying, "I finished as quickly as I could."

"I don't mind," she said, and pulled her hand away.

No doubt about it. Dr. Dean was dangerous. She was used to physical danger, used to the worry of some street snitch giving her up to the cops, used to gang toughs trying to take down A.A. as some sort of stupid initiation rite, but she had no idea how to deal with emotional danger. No idea how to stop herself from liking a man. She wondered for the first time if she was protecting him because it would thwart her enemy, or because she couldn't bear to see him hurt.

Supper was delightful. Jared noticed Kara ordered everything he did and wasn't sure why. Was it a sign of respect, or a lack of imagination?

He asked her. She made an exasperated sound and salted her fries. "Nice question. Lack of imagination, of course. The truth is, since you won't let me pay my way, I didn't want to bankrupt you by ordering three steak dinners."

"But I could be rich," he said, watching her long fingers as they curved around her burger and lifted it to her mouth. "Filthy, disgustingly rich."

"And we're eating at Denny's?" She took a bite, chewed, swallowed, then said with finality, "You're not rich at all."

"How do you—oh, cripes. You cracked the hospital personnel files, didn't you?" He let his head fall into his hands. "Did you leave any of the benefits staff conscious?"

"There aren't a lot of them around at two A.M." Then, almost anxiously, she added, "I wasn't snooping. I wanted to find out about you before I decided to get further involved. And by the way, did you know a good secretary makes more than you do in this city?"

"That's a lie. A mediocre secretary makes more than I do. Doctors don't make the bucks until they've been in the field for a while. Hell, six years ago I was still in med school."

"Taking your cadavers out to lunch," she added, smiling at him.

"It helped pass the time." He stretched in the booth, glancing around the restaurant. It was a typical Denny's, only a third full this time of the evening, and around them the muted clink of silverware on plates mingled with customer chatter.

It was a relief to be relaxed with Kara. He could look into her blue eyes without fantasizing about knocking their Fiesta burgers to the floor and taking her on the table while the waitress gaped and asked if they wanted anything else to drink. They could have a normal conversation. Well, as normal as a conversation about her cracking the hospital's confidential files could be.

Their thwarted lunch had helped. The nap she'd talked him into last night had also helped. But the raging hard-on he woke with had not. Neither had that weird-ass dream. Perhaps knowing Kara was in the next room, barely twenty feet away, made the stiffness between his legs demand urgent attention. Maybe it was the fact that he had thought of nothing and no one else for the past three days.

He had stumbled to the shower, still half asleep, and beneath the warm spray replayed their first— and, since he was keeping score, their only—kiss, only this time instead of pushing him away she had been pulling at his clothes. In his mind, her slender fingers tugged at his belt buckle, slipped his zipper down, her small, hot hand eased into his boxers and clasped him, caressed him, while she whispered in his ear exactly what she expected him to do to her the moment she was finished with him.

He had climaxed so hard his knees had buckled. Only then did he notice the water had turned cold. With a yelp, he had leaped past the curtain, standing on the bathroom carpet shivering, freezing, feeling more than a little foolish—but temporarily sated.

Now, finally, her power over him had eased. Here they were, having a conversation about med school cadavers like two ordinary people, and he was fine. Sure, a mob boss had put out a contract on his life and Kara was the only thing between him and a baseball bat lobotomy, but the fact remained, all was well with the world.

"I really think we should get married someday," he said, and nearly bit his tongue.

She rolled her eyes. "Always joking."

"Yup, that's me, Joke Central." Cripes, what was wrong with him? He was sated, her hold over him was purely physical, and she had no power over him, dammit, so what was wrong? She'd turned his life upside down in less than a week, he didn't know anything about her, but she was all he could think about, dream about.

He mentally shook himself, then looked at her to ask if she wanted dessert, and that was when she did it again. Her gaze flicked past him, to the front door, and then back to him. Her expression was neutral; if she had been any other woman he wouldn't have been alarmed. But Kara, he was beginning to realize, hid strong emotions—fear, anger, passion—behind an icy mask and he didn't like the way she kept glancing over his shoulder.

He turned and saw nothing out of the ordinary. Some new customers, but it was getting close to dinnertime and that was to be expected. He turned back to ask Kara what was going on, only to realize with a start that she had already gotten up and was strolling unhurriedly toward the front door. At her place was thirty dollars in cash.

"Wait!" he said, grabbing her money off the table and digging frantically for his wallet. "I said this was on me, remember?" He opened his wallet to find a movie ticket stub and two quarters peeping up at him. Dammit! No time to get cash yesterday and he'd been planning to pay for lunch with a credit card. With a muffled curse, he tossed her money back on the table and started after her.

He caught up with her as she was entering a dingy park across the street. The park was so small it was hardly the width of a city street, with a pitiful swing set and a teeter-totter that looked like it could deal death to unwary toddlers. The sodden sandbox was full of mud and a squatting cat, doing what Jared didn't want to think about. But the park, he saw with alarm, had one advantage for an ambush—trees pressed in closely on all sides but one and hardly anyone could see them from the street.

"What the hell is going—" was as far as he got

before Kara seized his arm, kicked over a park bench, and forced him behind it.

"Stay down," she said firmly, "and out of the way."

"What am I, your dog? You're not the boss of me. I . . . " He trailed off as Kara spun to deal with the accountants who had been following them.

He recognized the men. They had been, he realized, the last customers to take seats in the restaurant. They must have followed him and Kara right out the door into the park. There were three, all average-looking men with ordinary builds, nice suits, and expensive haircuts. Before he could figure out just when Kara had gone crazy and started attacking business executives, he noticed the one closest to her had his hand stiffened in a wicked-looking chop. Kara ducked under the blow and kicked the man high up on the ribs. Jared winced as the evil accountant bent, whooshing for breath and cradling his side.

The second one groped in his pocket and whipped out a pen—but it wasn't a pen, it was a three-foot-long antenna that whistled through the air like a blade. Kara reached out almost casually, and at the same time she caught the guy's wrist, she brought her knee crashing into his groin. But the third one was flanking her, moving past Kara's sight line and awfully close to Dr. Jared Dean, ER resident and pissed-off would-be boyfriend. The creep was going to whack *his* Kara?

"Mistake!" he yelled, as he shoved the park bench over. It caught Bad Guy #3 just behind the knees, effectively tumbling him face first to the damp ground. Jared pounced, and in midair imagined himself landing on the bad guy's back, forcing the air out of his lungs, and reigning triumphant.

Instead, the man flipped over quick as a snake, and as Jared's knees thudded to the ground on either side of Kara's assailant, a walloping pain exploded in Jared's nose.

He clapped both hands to his face, tasting blood and wondering dazedly when the bad guy had had time to throw a punch. As the man reared to a sitting position, Jared brought his head forth in a crude but effective head butt. *Now,* he thought with grim humor, *there's two of us holding our faces and thinking about throwing up.*

Hard fingers seized his ear and hauled him straight up. "Putz!" Kara hissed, just before she kicked Jared's bad guy in the chin, snapping his head back into the dirt. Jared looked around blearily and noted with no real surprise that Kara's two assailants were down for the count.

"Are you talking to me?" he asked thickly, then spat to clear his throat. "And let go of my ear, will you?"

"How did you ever get your medical license if you can't. Follow. Directions." Without a look at the unconscious men, she was marching Jared out of the park, across the street, back to his apartment. She never let go of his ear. She never stopped scolding him in a furious whisper. Finally, he reached up and pried her fingers loose.

"Back off, blondie," he said crossly. "If you expect me to cower behind a damned bench while you get set upon, you need some new medication."

"I expect you to do as you're told," she growled. They were now standing outside his apartment door and Jared fumbled tiredly for his keys. Before he could produce them, Kara yanked at her sleeve, produced two thin blades, and in about six seconds had his front door unlocked. He realized dazedly that it took him longer to unlock the door with a key than it took her to pick the lock. *Three cheers*, he thought, *for American ingenuity*.

She marched him inside, toward the bathroom. "I can't adequately protect you if you insist on throwing yourself in the path of danger. What's the matter with you? Any five-year-old knows enough to keep his head down and let the other person take the lumps."

"Bull*shit*," he replied politely. He found himself leaning against the sink while she ran warm water in the basin, found a washcloth, and gently pressed it to his nose and mouth. The tender motion was a puzzling conflict with her tight-lipped expression, narrowed eyes, and sharp words.

"Where I come from, you don't let the lady take the lumps. Jeez, what kind of household did you grow up in, any—" He made himself stop talking and stared at her. She was tending to his face and wouldn't look at him and no wonder—Kara hadn't exactly been brought up in the be-kind-to-children-and-animals mode.

"Putz," she said again, and he silently agreed.

A long moment passed, then he caught her wrists and gently took the washcloth away from her. "I can do that. And quit manhandling me, will you? Don't make me kick your ass."

She snorted and he continued. "Listen. I get that you're truly angry with me. I couldn't figure out why until right now—you truly feel it's your job to get hurt and mine to stay safe?" She said nothing. "The thing is, I see us as more of a team."

"We're not a team. I'm never in a team," she said fiercely, and tried to take the washcloth away from him. He held it high above her head, out of reach.

"Stop me if you've heard this before, but bullshit."

"I can't keep you safe if you're not going to listen," she said flatly. She gave him a disgusted look as he dangled the washcloth out of her reach, as if saying: *You don't really think I'm going to jump for that, do you?*

"Well, I won't stay safe if it means you'll get hurt. Period. The end. The fat lady singeth."

She stared at him. "You're an idiot."

He raised an eyebrow at her and sponged the rest of the drying blood off his face. The nosebleed had stopped a few minutes ago, luckily. "I don't want to see you get pounded, ergo I'm an idiot? What, you've never hung around with one of the good guys before?"

"I've never hung around with a moron before," she muttered, looking away.

He caught her chin and gently forced her to

look at him. "In all the excitement," he said mildly, although his heart was starting to pound, "I forgot to thank you for kicking some major ass on my behalf."

He leaned forward to kiss her and to his amazement and pleasure she met him more than halfway. She tenderly licked his sore upper lip, then her tongue slipped past his teeth and suddenly he was tasting her, devouring her, holding her tightly against his chest and kissing her with all the passion and excitement she had called up in him from the moment he first saw her.

Jared, who'd been sure the infatuation was one-sided, was thrilled to feel Kara's hands slip under his shirt, her fingers brushing across his nipples and sliding through his chest hair.

He cupped her head in his hands tenderly, carefully, as if holding a Fabergé egg, precious and priceless. He pulled at the clip keeping her hair up. Suddenly the rich blond waves were tumbling past his hands. He groaned and buried his face in her hair.

"Oh, we can't," she said in one breath, then nipped at his ear with her small teeth.

"We hardly know each other," he agreed with a groan, and kissed her throat. He brought his hands down to her waist, across her taut stomach, and up under her T-shirt. He closed his eyes and rubbed his face against her hair like a cat, for Jared Dean was a pure sensualist and nothing was more delightful to him than the feel and smell of a woman's skin and hair.

He explored her body as a blind man would, bringing his palms across the muscles in her abdomen, sliding up, marveling at the sleek power contained in her body. He found her bra and—hooray!—realized the clasp was in front; with one sure tug the fabric parted and her breasts were in his hands. He groaned again at the sheer joy of it, of her. Firm and sweet and fitting exactly into his palms, he caressed the tender undersides with his knuckles, then brought his thumbs to her nipples. She moaned and pressed against him as he stroked the stiff peaks, then kissed him so hard his lips flattened against his teeth. He had time for a dazed thought—*Did I ever think this woman was a cool one?*—before she was tugging at his shirt so hard, he could hear the buttons popping off and clattering on the bathroom tile.

"That's right, you're strong, rip our clothes off, rip *all* of our clothes off," he mumbled in delirious joy. "Take me, I'm yours." Her soft laughter brought a silly, pleased grin to his face.

She started to lean forward to kiss his now bare chest, but he stopped her long enough to pull her shirt over her head. Her bra straps were sliding off both shoulders but he couldn't take the time to help her out of it; he was transfixed by the perfection of her upper body. Slim, yet sleekly muscled, with proud, high breasts, her nipples were the dark pink of prairie roses and he would have gladly traded his medical license for a taste. Praise all the gods who ever were, he didn't have to. He kissed one, then licked, then sucked, pressing the nipple

63

to the roof of his mouth and tightening his grip at her sigh.

His arms were around her waist, then slid lower to cup her firm buttocks and pull her gently against his groin. She pushed back and he loosened his grip at once, but to his delight she wasn't pulling away, just trying to get more room. It was then that he noticed his nimble-fingered Kara had gotten his fly unbuttoned and his zipper down without him noticing.

And then her fingers were curving around his shaft, gripping him with cool and delicious friction, and he had time for one distracting thought— *God, don't let this be another fantasy*—before gladly giving in to the sensation. Kara's fingers, which slipped past locks and dealt blows hard enough to fell grown men, were the sweetest of dreams as she caressed, stroked, squeezed.

"OhKaraGod," he gasped, then brought her breasts together and ran his tongue along her cleavage as her breathing harshened and her fingers ran across his now slippery tip. He groaned and managed to stop himself from squeezing the pale globes until he marked her with his fingers. He wanted to mark her. He wanted to kiss and suck every inch of her body, leave a ring of hickeys around her throat like a necklace, wanted to write his name on her forehead with a laundry marker, wanted to marry her so she would be his forever, and he hers. Instead, he stopped himself from squeezing and attacked the button fly of her jeans. Being a fumble-fingered physician, his technique wasn't nearly as stealthy as hers. She didn't, thank God, seem to mind.

"More."

"Yes."

"I want—"

"That's so good—"

"Yes, you—"

"You—"

"Oh yes—"

He didn't know who was saying what, didn't care, it didn't matter. The only things in the world were her breath, her skin, her face, her sweet, courageous self.

"I've got to . . . got to send him a thank you note," he managed, then kissed her again.

"Who?" She said the word into his mouth, then lightly bit his lower lip and squeezed his throbbing dick with perfectly even pressure from each finger, stopping just short of pain, making him want to beg her to do that again. "Who?"

Who indeed? What the hell had he been talking about? Oh yeah . . . "Carlotti. One Eyebrow. The wonderful thug who brought you into my life. I'll send him flowers. Wash his car for a year. Something."

He felt the change in her at once. One instant she was warm and willing and had her hands all over him. The next, she was letting go, looking at him with eyes full of fright, then, in the next instant, eyes that showed nothing except cool waiting.

"That's enough of that," she said calmly, and gently pushed him back.

"Guh," he said, conscious of the fact that most of the blood his brain used was currently residing in his dick and, as such, he was definitely having trouble keeping up. "Wha . . .?"

"Sorry about that. We shouldn't mix business with, uh, other things. Why don't you zip up and join me in the living room?"

"Why don't we have sex on the bathroom floor instead?" he asked in what he hoped was a reasonable tone, but what he was afraid sounded dangerously low and rough with lust. He felt growing anger and stomped on it. No meant no, of course, but he could easily have strangled her. Had he ever been so aroused? Not since the night he lost his virginity—and maybe not even then.

"No thanks."

"The kitchen floor? The living room? The fire escape? The hallway? The corner diner? Where?"

"Get dressed," she said, not unkindly, and left the room.

# Chapter 4

Stupid. Stupid. Stupid. The thought thundered through her brain, even as she cupped her breasts, even as she ached for more of Jared's mouth and hands. She had nearly let him take her. "Let him"—ha! She had nearly raped him in his own damned bathroom, that was how badly she wanted him. He was all that was good and she was exactly the opposite, and why oh why couldn't she keep that in mind?

Kara fastened her bra, pulled her shirt back over her head, and sat down on the couch, dreading the moment Jared would come out of the bathroom. She'd abused him dreadfully, bringing them both to the edge then backing off and walking out without so much as a "Sorry, I'm not that kind of girl." She wouldn't have been surprised if he'd wanted to slap her. She was so disgusted with herself she would have stood still for it.

But only once.

She tried to pull her hair into a ponytail with trembling fingers, then remembered the clip was still in the bathroom and gave up. "Remember the rules," she said softly, trying to soothe herself, calm herself. Her voice sounded hoarse and she cleared her throat and went on silently, trying for calm. Usually she didn't have to try. *People you care for die or leave. Sometimes they can help it and sometimes they can't. Either way, it's better—safer—to never show true feelings. Don't get close. Don't get personal. You stupid cow.*

Scolding herself usually made her smile. Not this time. She had used Jared badly and owed him an explanation she would never let him hear— that she was powerfully drawn to him, that she would take a knife in the kidney before seeing him hurt, that she wished they could be together. Might as well wish she wasn't a carbon-based life form.

Jared walked into the room and tossed her hair clip at her, gently underhand. At least he hadn't fired it at her face with all his strength. She caught the clip and immediately pushed her hair up into it. She couldn't look at him.

"It's my breath, isn't it?"

Startled, she looked up and opened her mouth to reply. *Might have known he'd turn it into a joke,* she thought ruefully, and on the heels of that, *You're not worthy to be sitting on his couch, much less putting your hands on his body, so keep it in mind, okay, doll?*

He held up his hands. Skilled hands, healer's hands. Lover's hands. She tried not to stare at his fingers. "No, no, you can tell me. I won't be mad, I promise. Too many onions on my burger, right? I can take it." He grinned at her, that crooked smile she was starting to love.

"I'm sorry," she said. She looked up at him helplessly. "I don't have an explanation."

"That's okay, I do." He flopped down beside her and put his feet on the coffee table with a satisfying thump. She wanted to snuggle into him, the warmth of his body. Instead, she stared at the carpet. "You're secretly in love with me and couldn't help yourself. Or you've been heavily medicated for some time and need new drugs. Or you lost a bet. Or—"

"You're very nice," she interrupted, patting his thigh and then snatching her hand away. His thigh was long and heavily muscled; she wondered what he did to stay in shape. She wondered what he would think if she kissed him where her hand had just been. "But you're not for me."

"Not for you? What, like I'm something you'd pick up at Macy's?"

"Not Macy's," she said, hating her cool tone but helpless to stop. "Maybe Kmart."

His eyebrows arched. "Mee-yeow! Hey, don't take it out on me because you're sexually frustrated, sweetie. I was all set to tango . . . *you* were the one who called time out. Aarrggh!" He clutched his head, writhing. Alarmed, she reached for him, then forced her hand to drop back to her lap.

He looked up and speared her with his direct gaze. "I don't want to fight. Listen, I only kissed you because I couldn't stand being near you and not touching you. And because I really did want to thank you for taking care of the bad guys in the park. That's twice you've saved my butt. You barely know me and you keep putting yourself in danger for me. It's maddening, but sexy as hell." He picked up her hand and she let him, afraid to speak, afraid to return the pressure of his fingers. "Why are you doing this? Why me?"

"I don't know," she said.

"Well, I do," he said with maddening assurance. "It's because you're good, you couldn't stand to see someone in trouble and had to help. You—"

She flung off his hand and jumped up. "I'm *not* good!" she practically shouted. "I'm as far from good as someone like you could imagine."

His eyebrows arched. "Someone like me?"

She ignored the interruption. "I'm helping you because you've got a nice body and great eyes, okay? I'm in it for purely selfish reasons, I'm—I'm planning on shoring up your gratitude and trading it for sex, I—stop *laughing*."

He had actually fallen off the couch, was holding his stomach and giggling like an idiot. He choked off his mirth and said, "Sure you are. That's why you bolted out of my bathroom like your hair was on fire. 'Fess up, Kara. Why are you here?"

"A very good question," she grumbled, and stepped over him to leave. Damned if she was going to tell him a thing. Not that she had been planning to. But if she had been—and she had *not* been—she wouldn't now. No way. The man turned everything into a joke. She couldn't bear it if he turned her life into a punch line. "I'll see you tomorrow. Don't leave your apartment until I come back."

He rolled over, cat-quick, and grabbed her lower leg. Her progress toward the door slowed dramatically as she found herself lugging his two hundred pounds. "No you don't," he grunted. "You're not doing one of your Batman-type fadeouts. We're going to have a real talk like two people in a relationship."

"We're not in a relationship." She braced herself and pulled, with no luck. He was stuck to her leg like a lamprey. She had no leverage. She could have loosened his grip any number of ways—kicking him in the eye would be a good start—but couldn't bring herself to hurt him. Not physically, anyway. "Let go. Before I *put you in traction*."

"I'll call that bluff, thanks. Bodyguards don't whup their clients. Besides, we both know you're crazy about me." He chortled over what he probably assumed was a gross exaggeration. "Now talk! Who are you? Why are you here? When are you going to marry me?"

She stopped pulling and looked down at him. He was sprawled behind her, holding onto her calf with white knuckles. "Stop joking."

"I'm not," he said quietly. "I think you're fabulous. I want to be with you all the time. You're beautiful and smart and tough and vulnerable and sweet and a fantastic kisser and you have the prettiest breasts I've ever—"

"Stop it! You don't know me, you don't know anything about me, now *let me go.*"

He did and slowly got to his feet. But she had lost the urge to flee. "There's something else I know about you," he said. "You're scared shitless, but I'll be damned if I know what could scare *you.*"

*Complete rejection, for a start. Being left alone—again.* She pushed the thought away. "Jared, I've told you this before. If you knew me, knew who I really was—what I've done, the things I've—you wouldn't like me. You wouldn't want to be anywhere near me." She shuddered. "Sometimes I can't stand to be in my own skin."

He yawned. She gaped. "Yeah, yeah, you're a real badass, worse than Manson and Bundy put together."

Shocked, she opened her mouth to say . . . what, she didn't know, but he never gave her a chance. "Hey, you don't have to tell me a damned thing about yourself if you don't want to. Like you've said, this is business, right? That's assuming you don't have feelings for me. Which I would have believed before you let me put my hands all over your luscious bod."

"That's not—"

"You weren't faking, any more than I was—you feel the same thing I do. The connection. The heat." He poked her in the chest, an umpire making a point to the pitcher. "Difference is, *I'm* willing to admit it. You've been running away from it for days. So which one of us is the fearless body-guard and which of us is the coward?" He sighed, while she stared at him, stunned. "Too bad, so sad. I didn't think you were scared of anything or anyone. So disappointing to be wrong about people you care about."

Kara forced her fist to unclench. *It's not nice to punch doctors, no matter how outrageously provocative their comments,* she reminded herself. "You don't know anything," she snapped. "And you don't care about me."

They were nose to nose, or as close as they could get, as she was a head shorter. "Don't tell me how I feel," he growled. "You're fabulous, dammit, and that's the end of it."

"You don't even *know* me." Her voice cracked with desperation. "Jared, if you knew what I did for a living, the things I had to do to survive, you wouldn't feel this way."

His finger came to rest on the tip of her nose. He didn't smile. "Prove it."

There was a long silence and then she said it, ignoring the way her heart was pounding crazily, the way her head was screaming, *Are you out of your mind?!*

"You got it, Dr. Dean."


"Uh, Kara."
"Shhhhh."
"Kara. This isn't my house. Or yours."

"No talking."

"So this is breaking and entering."

"Well, yes. Technically."

"Technically?" he nearly shouted, then remembered he didn't want to go to jail and lowered his voice. "We're standing inside a house the size of the Playboy Mansion—"

She snickered. "That's not far off."

"—and I don't even want to know how you cracked that lock. Now there's little red lasers all over the living room, starting about two feet from where we're standing."

"It's the security system. Don't walk in there yet."

"Duh," he said with heavy sarcasm. "And now you're futzing with the alarm. Do you think they'll let me kiss you good-bye before they cart me off to the local hoosegow?"

She ignored him, simply popped the cover off the alarm plate and hooked up a small silver box, about the size of an ATM card. She crossed a few wires, then numbers started to stream across the digital display. A few seconds later, the lasers shut off.

"Cake," she said, brushing by him. "Don't touch anything."

"Thanks. Maybe you should remind me to keep breathing and any other obvious advice you can think of." He followed her nervously. Prove it, he'd said, and she had taken him right up on it. *Your own fault, moron.*

He'd suspected nothing when she drove them to the house. Hell, he hadn't even noticed they'd left his own modest neighborhood for the more pretentious Carleton area, where mansions were as plentiful as street lamps. He'd spent the drive trying to figure out a way to prove to her that her past and her current activities didn't change the way he felt about her. Hell, her past had shaped the woman he was falling in love with. Far from scaring him off, it just made him feel closer to her.

He was close to her right now, in fact. So close he could have strangled her, which he felt like doing. This was big-time trouble if they were caught. They were both looking at prison terms for the evening's exercise, all so Kara could prove she was a criminal sociopath.

"I thought you said we were going hacking," he muttered, following her through the mansion. "I pictured us in a cozy computer room somewhere, pressing buttons. Not hanging around in a living room that looks like it was decorated by the director of the Guggenheim."

"Hacking doesn't have much to do with computers these days." She was climbing the stairs slowly, steadily, not looking back. "It's B&E-speak for getting into a business to steal from it."

"But this is somebody's house. Thirty or forty somebodies, given the size, but still . . ."

"It's a business," she said with maddening mysteriousness and wouldn't continue, no matter how much he kept bugging her.

Although the house was empty, the owners had left several lights on, shattering another of Jared's theories about burglaries. Kara wasn't a twitchy junkie with a heroin habit to feed, the "breaking" of the breaking and entering took about ten seconds, and nothing was broken, and there were lights all over the place, so no creeping in the dark like a demented boogeyman. Jared wondered what else popular fiction had wrong about crime.

The bedroom was a joke. Something out of a bad movie—a bed the size of his kitchen, covered with a red satin comforter and about a thousand pillows. Mirrored ceiling. Dark furniture the owner's family probably brought to America via the *Mayflower.* The carpet—cream shag—was so deep, he could feel himself actually sink into it. The dressers were spotless, except for one large picture of a middle-aged white male, bearded and benevolent looking, with a smile so large, it showed his back teeth. The guy looked like Santa on acid. And, if this was his house, it was kind of in bad taste to have the only photo in the bedroom be of himself.

*Bad taste,* Jared thought with grim humor, *sure. Almost as bad as breaking into someone's house.*

There were mirrors everywhere. It was like being trapped in a carpeted disco. Jared could see seven reflections of himself and seven Karas stepping up to a mirror and doing something. And then the mirror was swinging open and . . .

"Jesus!"

They were in a vault. Kara, her fingers safe in surgical gloves, was opening a drawer and withdrawing a necklace worth, he estimated, the GNP of China.

"You can't steal that," he said, trying to sound authoritative, but very much afraid he was whining.

She smiled at him like a cat. It was irritating, he thought, how beautiful she looked even when she was being sly. "Can't I? If you mean I don't have the ability, you're wrong. If you mean my moral code won't let me, you're wrong. If you mean I'll go to jail, you're wrong again."

"If I mean it's rotten, I'm right. Put it back." She moved to tuck the necklace away and he grabbed her wrist. She raised an eyebrow at him and looked pointedly at his hand, but he didn't loosen his grip. "Look, you've made your point. I see what you do now."

"Do you?"

"You're terrible, awful, evil, a real blight on society, I should have listened to you back at the apartment, blah blah. But don't steal from these folks just to prove me wrong."

"Open the last drawer on the left," she said quietly. "Use your shirt sleeve, don't leave prints."

"Look, I don't care how much jewelry they—"

She pried his fingers off her wrist. "Just open it, please, Jared."

He did. At first his eyes wouldn't translate what he was seeing. When they did, he blindly put his hand out for something to lean on, certain he was about to be sick. Kara was there, not letting him touch anything, letting him sag against her.

"Those men—"

"And children, yes."

"Filthy goddamned perverts!"

"Yes, and they're having terrible luck," she said sympathetically. He stared at her; she sounded genuinely sorry for them. "The film from their last drop-off was intercepted by the cops. And now they've been robbed. When the cops come, they'll find . . . this."

In a flash, he saw her brilliance, saw the trap she had lain for the pedophiles. "The police can't search without a warrant," he said slowly, "but if there's a robbery . . . and they happen to find pictures, say, all over the hallway . . ." He paused. "But you're never caught."

She grinned at him. "We're going to trip the alarm on the way out. Cops'll be here in about five minutes." She opened another drawer full of filth and waved a spare pair of surgical gloves at him. "Want to help?"

"That was fun," he said half an hour later, feeling more deeply satisfied than he ever had. Saving lives was fabulous, but preventing the further brutalization of children was even better. "Now where are we? Is it time for ice cream?"

"Pross house," she said shortly, getting out of the car and striding, unafraid, through the worst neighborhood in the city. There were more streetlights out than on, more shattered store windows than whole, and entirely too many rough-looking men giving *his* Kara the once-over. Jared could feel himself bristling and singled out the meanest-looking one for a good glare. "Keep up, please."

"I don't like the looks of those guys," he said, nodding to a gang of thugs clustered under a broken streetlight. "You want I should rough 'em up for you?"

She laughed. "Aren't you cute. Jared, trust me. Worry about the ones you *don't* see."

She bounded up the steps to a battered brownstone, nodding politely to two teens—either of which could have given your average beat cop a run for her money—and ringing the buzzer. The teens appeared to completely ignore her, but Jared noticed they both made way. He reached out and snagged Kara's elbow just as she was buzzed in. "I'm with her," he told the teens, who ignored him as they had Kara, "and don't get smart or I'll have her whup you both."

Inside, he was pleasantly surprised to find a homey entryway. Shabby, but dignified. "Well, this is something," he said, looking around. "First, the Playboy Mansion. Then the fence—that's the guy who cashed in the necklace, right? Now we're . . . I have no idea where. What's a pross house?"

"This isn't a pross house," a warm, pleasant voice said. Jared jumped and spun; Kara turned unhurriedly toward the voice and Jared realized Kara had known they weren't alone in the hall. "That's a place where prostitutes, ah, ply their trade. This is a shelter for soiled doves trying to make new lives for themselves."

The woman who spoke was astonishingly beautiful, despite the knife scar that bisected her right cheek. Far from detracting from her beauty, the scar served to accent the flawless state of the rest of her face. She had shoulder-length, rich brown hair the color of dark chocolate, eyes the color of a sea lagoon, and skin the color of a really good espresso. She was quite a bit shorter than Kara and if she weighed more than a hundred pounds, Jared vowed to eat the scale.

"Ma'am," he said politely.

"Madam, actually," she said, and tittered. "Well, former madam. But you know."

"Present for you, Meg." Kara handed her the shoe box in which, Jared knew, there nestled close to half a million dollars.

"Awwww . . ." Meg caught the box and tucked it under her arm like a football. "And I didn't get you anything. Who's the stiff stud?"

"I happen," he said with as much dignity as he could muster, "to be the young lady's personal physician. I started by advising her that this neighborhood is bad for her health but—"

Meg brayed laughter, cutting him off. "Her? There's nothing in this neighborhood bad for A.A. She's safer here than anywhere."

*Click.* Everything fell into place. But instead of being shocked, he felt like nodding thoughtfully. Shocked? Hell, he wasn't even mildly surprised. The only reason he hadn't figured it out earlier was, he'd always thought A.A.—whenever he thought about A.A. at all—was more interested in lining his or her pocket than protecting doctors from hitmen.

Kara turned to leave. "I'll see you, Meg."

"I know. Can't stay away, can you? Good for us." Meg's smirk switched off and she abruptly looked haggard, old. "Bad for you."

Kara shrugged and left without another word. Jared offered his hand to Meg, who only looked at it, amused. Then he hurried after Kara.

"I've got it," he said on the street.

"Whatever it is, put it back," she said reasonably, opening the car door and sliding inside.

Jared realized with a start that she hadn't bothered to lock the car—and it had remained unmolested the entire time they were inside. Well, no wonder. Given who she was.

"You're the Avenging Angel," he said, jumping into the passenger seat. "I've read about you. You've been doing a Robin Hood thing, stealing from the rich and corrupt, then donating the money to homeless shelters and such." He felt like clapping, he was so pleased at having figured it out. Then it hit him and he didn't feel like clapping anymore. "But this is terrible."

"I warned you," she said quietly, driving back to his apartment.

"This is why you can't testify against ol' One Eyebrow. The D.A. is at least as interested in putting you in jail as he is some mob hood. Jesus, there's—didn't I read somewhere that there's a five-hundred-thousand-dollar reward for your capture? The guys you've been stealing from put up a pot?"

She didn't say anything.

"Well, hell, this is totally unacceptable! The D.A. should *thank* you, not issue warrants for your arrest."

She looked at him. In the poorly lit car, all he could see were her eyes. They were huge. He tried not to yelp as she ran a red light. "What?" she whispered. "What did you say?"

"I said, why don't you let me drive? Seriously. Kara? What's the matter?"

She didn't answer. He didn't get another word out of her until they were back at the apartment.

# Chapter 5

"I'll pick you up tomorrow." She glanced at her watch. "Later this morning, I mean."

He folded his arms across his chest. "Forget it. You're coming inside with me so we can finish talking about this."

She snorted. He looked so stubborn, so determined. It was cute, if irritating. "Don't make me throw you out of this car, Jared. I'd try not to hurt you, but you wouldn't like it, just the same."

He wasn't, she saw with surprise, fazed by her threat. "If you do, I'll stand on the street corner, waving my arms and telling everyone that Carlotti is the only man on the planet with penis envy. That he used to have two eyebrows but quit plucking them when his tweezers broke. That I saw him assaulting my future wife and I'm going to tell the world, take out an ad, camp out in the D.A.'s office. How long do you think it'd take for him to come get me?"

She stared at him. Her throat had actually gone dry; she swallowed to force moisture. "You wouldn't— never mind. You're crazy enough to do it. Fine. We'll go in."

Once inside, he absently locked the front door—not that it would do any good against anyone like her—took their jackets, and tossed them on the couch. She turned her back to him and wondered, once again, if she had lost her mind. What was she thinking, showing this straitlaced doctor a piece of her life? And why hadn't he thrown her out, or at least threatened to turn her in? He'd pretended to be appalled because the D.A. wanted her arrested, not because she stole for a living, and that was the biggest, most vicious lie she'd heard from a man yet.

"So, what?" he was saying. "I figured it out, you're the notorious A.A. Was that my cue to scream and run away? To never see you again? Was that supposed to make me *not* attracted to you? Because it failed, failed, failed."

Anger at his obtuse nature flared in her and she gladly went with the emotion. She was tired of holding back, tired of forcing cool when he made her feel the exact opposite.

She slammed her hand on the back of the couch, kicking up a small puff of dust. "Jesus, don't you get it? I'm not like you, I'll *never* be like you. I can't live in your world and you certainly can't live in mine. I wanted to protect you from Carlotti until we neutralized him and that's fine, but that's all there is."

"The hell." He started toward her and she stumbled back, not trusting herself to stay strong, stay angry, if he touched her. If he touched her, she was going to forget all about their differences—again. "I see your little field trip for what it is. You broke into a mansion and did what you liked there—no one could stop you. Then you went to a fence, who sure isn't going to turn you in—he's probably been profiting off your hobbies for years. Then you take me to the worst neighborhood in the city to show me how everyone defers to you. This whole 'hacking' thing was supposed to prove that you're evil incarnate and—tell the truth—you *wanted* to show me what you could do. You wanted to show off a little. Don't you get that you don't have to steal to be worth something?"

"You don't understand, I knew you couldn't under—"

He swiftly crossed the room to her and put his hands on her shoulders, shaking her as one would a child. His face was blazing, but not with anger. With sincerity and passion. "You're precious in yourself, you need to prove nothing, you've got so much to offer, you are *your own self*, Kara, and you're not defined by what you steal or who you can beat up."

"I—that's not—"

"You think I care that you're a thief? You think I care that you steal pretty stones and give them to people who don't have your determination to stay strong? You think I give two shits that the D.A. wants to throw your ass in jail?" The mere act of

saying the words made Jared's expression darken.
"He won't, not while I'm around. Nobody is going
to put you in a cage while I'm around, so just stop
it, stop running away, stop pretending you don't
feel it, stop telling yourself you don't want me as
badly as I want you."

"I—"

He shook her again and the word was a roar.
"Coward!"

She brought them to the floor with a deft leg
sweep, landing squarely on top of his chest. He was
still holding her shoulders and she stared into his
eyes, dark and blazing. "I am a coward," she said
softly, less than an inch from his mouth, "but only
when I remember I have something to lose." Then
she bent down and kissed him. His arms were
around her a moment later, his mouth opening
beneath hers. "Thief," he said into her mouth.
"Took my heart, too, damn you."

*Then I'm not the only thief in the room,* she had time
to think, before capitulating to the sensations he
effortlessly called up in her. His crisp, clean, utterly masculine scent delighted her, she felt like
burying her face in his neck and never letting go.
She tugged at his shirt and his fingers were there,
frantically unbuttoning it for her, and then he was
yanking at her T-shirt. She sat up, straddling him,
and pulled it off, then unsnapped her bra. He
groaned as her breasts bounced free and reached
eagerly for her, his arms coming around her, his
fingers stroking the smooth skin of her back. He
sucked at the tender skin at the hollow of her

throat and she grinned, knowing a hickey would soon bloom there, realizing they were like a couple of horny teenagers, furiously necking on the living room floor. As a teenager, she'd never had the leisure to neck on anyone's floor. She found she liked it. A lot.

She pulled free of him and stood, then unzipped her jeans and slid them down her thighs until they puddled on the floor. He lay on the floor, arms crossed behind his head and watched with eyes narrowed from urgency. She pulled her panties down and stood over him for a long moment. His gaze held nothing but admiration, but part of her was frightened. It had been years since she had done this. Over three, at least, and the last time out of pure loneliness and desperation, a foolish one-night stand; she had never seen the man again.

But this was different, Jared was different. She hadn't had feelings for her other lovers, pitiful though their numbers were. She hadn't had to will herself to keep her hands off them, didn't feel deep fear in the pit of her stomach when one of them had been in danger. The three men she had taken out of loneliness since she turned seventeen had lived in her life, had been raised by the same institutions she had, and were quite conversant with danger. But Jared . . .

"I want you to know something," he said softly, breaking her tormented reverie.

"Yes, Jared?" Was she really standing naked over this man, debating whether or not to take him?

"Be gentle. It's my first time. Also, frequent exposure to X-ray radiation has neutered me."

"Oh!" She pounced on him, cutting off his laughter before it really got started. "How can you make jokes at a time like this?"

"I can't help it," he chuckled, "I joke when I get nervous. And since you looked like you were getting ready to bolt—naked, no less—I figured I'd better say something before you pulled another Houdini."

"Do me a favor and stop figuring," she said dryly and then he mock-grabbed for her. She pulled back and they rolled over and over on the floor, tussling. She won, of course, and soon she was once again straddling him.

"Has anyone ever told you how utterly, utterly gorgeous you are?" he said, his expression pure delight. She blushed at his obvious sincerity. "Someone should paint you and hang you in a museum."

"Museums, now there's an easy hack," she teased.

He groaned and put his hands under her bottom. For a moment she wondered if he was going to grab her, then realized he was shoving his jeans down. "Kara, please. Now is *not* the time. I don't want to hear how you cracked the Louvre and made off with a zillion dollar's worth of paintings."

"I was only kidding. I'd never steal from a museum," she said, offended.

"Of course. How silly of me." He stopped smiling when he saw she wasn't. "I know. You only crack the bad guys. Reason number seven hundred fifty-seven why I've got a crush on you the size of Czechoslovakia. Now come here."

She bent to him, still prepared to sulk, then realized she was looking for a reason, any reason, tempted to pick a fight, so she wouldn't have to be intimate with him. It wasn't a matter of being afraid of him. It was strictly a matter of being afraid of losing control, of blurting things to him that she swore to herself she would never tell anyone, ever.

His lips drove the unpleasant thoughts from her mind. They nibbled and kissed and sucked, and then his tongue was darting into the cup of her ear and she could feel the zing of pleasure right down to her toes. She could feel his length pressing urgently against her lower stomach and reached down to gently clasp him. He was hot and hard and quite large and throbbed intriguingly against her palm. She started to ease down, intent on taking him into her mouth, when he grabbed her shoulders and pulled her back up.

"Oh, no," he said softly. "I'm thrilled, honest to God, but if you do *that*, we're done before we started."

"How disappointing," she teased.

"Shameful, but true. I remember your fingers from the last time we got carnal, you know. You can get to anything . . . especially me." While he murmured to her his hands were on her breasts, his fingers gently caressing the sensitive undersides.

She stroked his stomach, his ribs, enjoying the

way his firm flesh felt beneath her hands. He liked to rave about her body, but he was in pretty fine shape himself. She told him so.

"Volleyball," he replied. "That's the secret. Also being too overworked to eat. Now come down here again. Kiss me."

She did, and as his tongue slipped past her teeth she felt his fingers caressing her stomach and moving lower. Straddling him as she was, her knees were spread wide and he found her easily. She sucked in a breath as his fingers stroked her slick flesh, moving with exquisite care and gentleness.

"Oh, that's nice. You're like . . . like hot damp silk," he sighed, breaking the kiss. One of his fingers slipped inside her, just barely nudging into her, and she swallowed a groan. "Sit up a bit so I can watch your face."

A terrifying thought. He could watch her unguarded expressions, know instantly just how dear his touch was, how she craved it, craved him . . . "No," she said, hoping he would mistake her breathlessness for passion and not apprehension.

His face didn't change but his eyes went thoughtful and his finger slowly withdrew. "Okay," he said easily, "that's all right." He pushed her up a bit and put his hands on her thighs, spreading them even wider. His thumbs stroked her inner thighs. "Kara, sweetheart, I'm dying to find out if you taste as good as you look." While he talked, his hands were easing her forward, his voice gentle, as if soothing a wild mustang ready to bolt. More than a little dazed by the magic his fingers had wrought, she found herself over his mouth. She put her hands out and steadied herself against the wall, and instantly realized that in this position he couldn't see her face. Why had he done that? What was he thinking?

Then his tongue flicked against her and darted up inside her and she forgot everything except how he was making her feel. She swallowed a groan as he gently kissed then sucked and nibbled her so sensitive flesh while marvelous warmth spread through her limbs, while she bit her lip to keep from crying out, while she pounded her palms against the wall. He groaned against her slick flesh and the vibration sent another shock wave of pleasure racing through her. She began to rock against his sweetly talented mouth, as unable to stop her movement as she could have regulated her heartbeat. Her orgasm neared, taunted her, then danced out of reach.

She felt his thumbs between her thighs, spreading her apart, exposing all of her to his mouth, and she nearly shrieked at the wonder of it. She should have felt laid open, vulnerable, frightened. Instead, she was very much afraid Dr. Jared Dean was going to be raped in another half minute if he didn't . . .

His tongue found her throbbing center, darted across the sensitive bud, and then his lips closed around it and he suckled gently while his tongue flicked with astonishing speed. She wasn't slapping the wall anymore, she was pounding it with her fists, her concentration narrowed to a fine point—in all the world, there was only his mouth and her approaching orgasm. But, ah God, it was still so far away, dancing just out of reach, she couldn't . . .

His finger—no, *two* fingers slid inside her, but his mouth, his tongue, never stopped and her orgasm wasn't far away at all, it was *right here*, racing through her, making her shake, making her choke back a wild groan, making her claw the wall.

Another few moments and she was resting her forehead against her arm, trying to get her gasps under control. "Jared," she breathed.

He was stroking her thighs; she'd pulled back from his mouth so he could have some breathing room. "Yes, hon?"

"Do it again," she whispered and smiled at his groan. He put light pressure on her thighs and she let herself be pushed down until she was straddling him again. She reached behind her and found him, clasped him gently. About to lower herself on his throbbing rod, a glance at his face told her how it was with him—there was a muscle jumping in his cheek and his eyes were dark slits. His "Yes, hon?" had been so thick as to be unrecognizable. That made her feel closer to him than the intimate duty he'd just performed for her. What was it he had said? That it was a relief to find out the attraction wasn't just one-sided?

"I want to go slowly," she said, "to make it last."

He nodded. "Sure. I see that happening." He pushed at her thighs and lunged; in half a second he was fully embedded inside her, his hot hard length starting a glorious aching inside her. "Sorry," he panted, while she gasped and steadied herself on his chest as he began to thrust, "but if I don't come soon I'm definitely going to enter heart attack country. *God*, you tasted good . . . sounded good."

She didn't care, she barely heard his words, she was astonished at the power of his strokes, how he manipulated both their bodies to give them pleasure, how in this instance he wasn't easygoing Dr. Dean, but a pure male animal, determined on his course, obeying a biological imperative older than the family of man.

She recovered from her surprise long enough to help him, to meet his thrusts, and they both moaned in unison at how splendid that was, how they both made each other feel. If she believed in such things, she would have thought their bodies had been made expressly for the other and no one else—certainly it had never been like this before with another man. How could it have been? Other men were not Jared.

He pulled her toward him and kissed her, and the taste of herself on his mouth coupled with the fierce plunging between her thighs jolted her into another orgasm; she whimpered into his mouth. His tongue thrust past her teeth, demanding, possessing, insisting, his hands were hard on the back of her neck, forcing her to him, keeping her to him, and she wanted more, needed more, but finally it was too much, too intense, and she broke the kiss and buried her face in his throat. He cradled her head gently and then stiffened, and she could feel his muscles lock as he at last found release.

They stayed pressed together for some minutes, too sated to venture conversation, but Kara started a silent countdown and couldn't help but smile when the inevitable wisecrack came—"You realize that as my bodyguard, it's completely unethical for you to be sexually harassing me like this? I'm lodging a complaint with the union."

"I knew you'd find a way to spoil this," she said, but she didn't mean it. "This" had been nothing special, not at all, merely an instant treasured memory to be taken out and lovingly explored sometime in the future when she was alone again. "Am I too heavy? Should I get off?"

"Yes, and don't you dare move. Christ. As much as I've been fantasizing about it, I never thought it'd be so fabulous."

She giggled into his neck. "You've been fantasizing? About me?"

"No, about Granny from *The Beverly Hillbillies.* Of course about you. Christ, don't you know? You're all I can think about. Dream about. Wait'll I tell you what I was reduced to doing in the shower this morning . . ."

"No thanks," she said dryly, inwardly thrilling to his words. "And as far as the sex being good, conceit, thy name is Jared. It was good because *you're* good." She laughed. "And it's obnoxious to immediately start complimenting your own performance."

"That's not it at all," he said, serious for once. She pulled back from his embrace and looked at him. There was no hidden grin, no teasing glint in his eyes. "It was you. You're amazing . . . so beautiful and responsive. Although," he added with a wry smile, "you certainly did your best to hide the fact that you were affected by my surging, tumescent loins—"

"Tumescent means windy," she said, fighting another laugh.

"I mean, would it have killed you to scream that I was your love monkey? Maybe claw my back a little?"

She didn't say anything, just kept smiling. Funny how he had noticed, though. Her control seemed to bother him, though she wasn't sure why. If anything, he should be grateful for it.

"Next time, maybe," he said, then leered when she raised her eyebrows at him. "Aw, you know you can't resist me, baby. Of course, I'll need a good forty-eight hours to recover . . ."

She poked him in the ribs, earning a grunt, then snuggled against him again, oddly reluctant to separate from him. Their lovemaking had been marvelous, sublime, but it had solved nothing. They were still ludicrously different, he would still bug out on her the moment things got hairy. But for now . . .

*For now*, she thought, *I could almost believe in happy endings.*

"Oh, Kara," he sighed, stroking her back, "you really do have to marry me."

She froze. He felt it at once, but didn't comment, just kept running his hands up and down her back, trying to calm her with his touch. She would have given anything to know what he was thinking.

*Stupid,* she told herself. *You know what he's thinking. Unlike you, he doesn't hide how he feels. He really thinks he loves you, the poor bastard.*

*O God,* she thought in despair, *we are in so much trouble.*

# Chapter 6

He fell asleep with a stupid grin on his face, a grin that absolutely would not fade. He didn't want Kara thinking he had some sort of "me Tarzan, you Jane, me Jane's hot love monkey" mentality about what they had shared, so he tried to quit smiling by deliberately calling up terrible thoughts. Famine (*Boy, Kara doesn't eat enough to keep a newborn alive, I should really get her to eat more . . .* ); war (*Kara would kick some major ass in a war, we should get her into Iraq, take care of a few problems that way . . .* ); working a forty-eight-hour shift with no intern to help (*I wonder if Kara would come to work with me again and hang out for a while?*). She pervaded every rotten thought, making every one of them not so rotten. And now she was sleeping beside him!

She hadn't wanted to. She'd wanted to get off the floor, get dressed, lock him in his apartment like a barely trained dog, and leave for the rest of the night. To go where, he had no idea—he didn't even know if she lived in the city. She was obviously rattled by his latest declaration of love and in true Kara fashion wanted to run away from strong emotion, hide until she had everything under control. Jared wanted more.

Seeing he was going to be stubborn, she had sighed and acquiesced and they had crawled into bed together. Kara had dropped off at once—after insisting she be the one to sleep nearest the door, still selflessly looking out for him like the utter sweetheart she was—but Jared was having a little more trouble.

Of course, *he* hadn't gotten into a fight, taken out three strong men, broken into a mansion, swung by a pross house, and then hotly defended her way of life, all in the space of six hours. All he'd done, as usual where she was concerned, was watch and make wisecracks. Except at the end of the evening, of course.

His smile broadened, remembering. Sliding between Kara's thighs, seeing her gaze soften as her body welcomed him, had been like coming home. In much the same way someone's life flashed before their eyes at the moment of death, in that instance their future flashed before his. He saw a wedding, Kara blooming with child, babies, a house in the country. Children blessed with his sense of humor and Kara's utter fearlessness. He saw, oh, everything he'd ever wanted since he was old enough to realize people could make their own families, their own happiness.

He knew better than to mention any of this to Kara. She got rattled enough when he told her he loved her. He always tried to make it sound like a joke, or hide the phrase in the middle of a sarcastic observation, but she tensed up anyway. No doubt about it—the woman he'd fallen for was big-time damaged.

Now, what to do about it?

*Also,* his mind whispered to him, annoyed, *there's a contract out on your life.*

Right, right, he hadn't forgotten. Well, actually he had, for hours. Getting to know Kara was infinitely more interesting than worrying about some mob boss who, frankly, Kara could beat the snot out of anytime she liked.

He glanced over at her, able to see quite well thanks to the moonlight splashed all over the room. Kara slept in the nude and her full breasts were peeking out from under the sheet. Her hair was unbound and spread across the pillow and looked as amazing as he had imagined it would. Interestingly, there was a frown wrinkle between her eyebrows, and even deep into REM sleep, she looked like she was thinking hard about how to get out of a trap.

He tucked an arm around her slender shoulders and pulled her toward him, and she at once shifted in her sleep and cuddled into his embrace. He smiled again—God, he just could not *stop* with the grinning—and thought it was telling that Kara didn't keep any sort of distance between them when she wasn't consciously trying.

Her thigh was draped across him and the feel of her smooth skin, coupled with the sweet weight of her breasts against his arm, caused an interested stirring between his legs. He forced the thought away. Kara needed her sleep—and so did he.

Now if he could only stop grinning.

Doctors, especially those not long out of their first year of residency, often came awake easily. In Jared's case, Kara's uneasy stirring brought him fully awake a moment before she cried out in her sleep. The sheets and blankets had twisted around her and she fought them with weak, frantic cries. He shook her shoulder—and dodged as her small fist shot out, missing the side of his face by a hair.

"Kara! Wake up, honey, you're having one hell of a bad dream."

"Everybody's gone!" she cried, thrashing. "They're gone, I'm all alone again. No! Come back! *Come back!*" The body was Kara's, the deadly fists were also hers, but the wailing was that of a child, abandoned. Lost. And Jared instinctively responded to that voice.

"That's not true," he soothed, dodging another flailing fist and pulling her into a tight embrace. "I'm here. You're not alone. Everything's all right." *Until she remembers a little more of her training,* he thought nervously, *and knees me in the gonads.*

Trembling like a puppy, she shook her head against his shoulder. He was fairly certain she wasn't awake—not completely—and wondered how old this memory of hers was. Ten years? Twenty? "They're all gone," she said, almost moaned, "and I have to go back. He'll hurt me. He's always hurting me."

Who, Jared wondered with growing rage, was "he"? A foster father? A guard at juvenile hall? One of the many who had hurt Kara for his own end, then either abandoned her or forced her to run away again. Only, Jared grimly deduced, to be brought back and shuffled into another foster home, where the cycle could start again. And again. A wretched existence, one that had broken more children than not. It was amazing that Kara had not only survived, but had emerged with her conscience and honor intact.

"No one lays a hand on you while I'm around," he said, pulling the blankets over both of them, gratified at how she pressed against him, already relaxing back into sleep. "It's all right. I'm here and I'm not going anywhere. Not ever."

*Not even,* he added silently, *if I have to handcuff myself to your side for a year to get you to believe I'd never abandon you.*

He caressed her breast, felt her nipple stiffen against his palm, and stroked slowly, soothingly. She sighed. "Go to sleep," he murmured, "there's nothing here to be scared of," and wondered how the hell *he* was supposed to go to sleep with a cock that was now wide awake and raring to go. *For starters, you could keep your hands to yourself, moron.*

Sure. He'd stop eating and breathing while he was at it.

Her eyes were open and she was staring at him in the gloom. She rolled closer, pressing more of her breast into his hand. She took a deep, shaky breath and let it out slowly. "Jared," she whispered, "don't stop."

"Was that 'Don't. Stop!' or 'Don't—'"

"Jared."

"Sorry."

"Just shut up," she said, not unkindly, "and love me."

"That's an easy one," he said gently, kissing her brow. "Easier than breathing." He wasn't talking about the physical act. He wondered if she knew that. Even if she did, he realized, she wouldn't believe him. It was enough to make him want to weep—or beat the living shit out of everyone in her life who had ever hurt her.

He forced that away, not wanting to let ugly thoughts intrude on their precious time together. He leaned forward and kissed her, slowly sucking her lower lip into his mouth. She made a small sound and reached for him, found him, then her hand slid lower and she gently cuddled his testicles in her palm.

He pressed kisses to her throat, her upper chest, her breasts, and moved lower, licking the small cup of her navel, nuzzling the sweet fleshy slope that led to her marvelous center. He parted her with his tongue, smiling at her gasp, and slowly, lovingly licked her slick length, tasting her salty warmth. She was still damp from their earlier love-making, from the seed he'd eagerly given her and that thought—he'd left his mark on her, in her—thrilled his inner Neanderthal.

She was wriggling while he nuzzled and licked and kissed, catching more and more of her wet-ness with his tongue, spreading her damp folds so he could lap up her marvelous juices. Wriggling and groaning and saying something and . . . mov-ing? He was so deeply into the moment, concen-trating on her so fiercely, that he hadn't noticed her movements until he felt her own mouth close around him. Her hand was still cupping his testi-cles, but now he could feel himself easing into her mouth, down her throat. In response he jabbed his tongue inside her as far as it would go and felt her tremble beneath him. In response to *that*, she backed off, only to slowly suck one of his testicles into her mouth.

He nearly fainted on the spot. It felt like the bot-tom dropped out of his scrotum. The sensation was so fine he could feel his eyes roll back. He couldn't recall any woman ever doing that to him before.

She eased off again, probably feeling him shak-ing like a mobile home in a hurricane, and whis-pered anxiously, "Was that all right? I've never tried that before."

He said something—"Gbbrrlldd," it sounded like—and when she tried it again his hips bucked

103

without prompting from his brain. She played with him like that for a while, her tongue dancing circles around his aching balls, and he endured, his face pressed against her inner thigh, not daring to pleasure her for fear he would accidentally bite her or be too rough. When she pulled back and again sucked his length into her mouth, he felt it was safe to continue with her and, in fact, was eager for the taste of her again.

She was holding him quite easily and he marveled at the concealed strength in her small, wiry frame. She was supporting him by his inner thighs, occasionally lowering him enough so he could plunge deeply into her throat, then pushing him back so she could breathe easier. While she took breaths, her tongue flicked out at the tip of him, teasing, stroking, and even—very gently—nibbling.

In response, he again spread her wide and licked her slick length, pausing to pay extra, delicate attention to the impudent bud that was the center of her pleasure. Her thighs trembled in his hands as he slowly sucked her clit into his mouth and he hummed against her flesh, knowing the vibrations would push her closer to the edge. He dipped a finger inside her, then withdrew, then dipped again. When his finger was slick, he stroked a path down to the tight bloom of her anus and gently rubbed the rich core of nerve endings there. She made a surprised sound which escalated to a muffled shriek as he slowly pushed his finger past that tight muscular ring. She writhed, trying to jerk away from him, but had no leverage from her position and, with his cock in her throat, no way to verbally protest.

"Easy," he murmured, "just let me . . . for another few seconds . . . it's all right . . ." When he was up to the first knuckle he bent to her again, jamming his tongue inside her damp cave and prodding as his nose dug into her clitoris and his finger slid around slowly, out just a touch and then in, no big dramatic strokes, just an overall pressure and gentle wriggling.

She quit trying to get away from him; he could, in fact, feel her entire body quaking as her orgasm neared. She let go of his thighs and he thrust against her warm, inviting mouth, hoping like hell she was getting enough air, hoping like hell he would come soon before he had a heart attack. Meanwhile, the taste and smell of her was in his mouth, his nose, driving him crazy, making him want to never stop touching her, tasting her, and she was bucking against him and he felt her clench around him as she shook with the force of her orgasm. A half-second later, he found his own release, felt his seed pouring down her throat and pulled back, afraid for her, but she held onto his thighs with an iron grip and milked him greedily, not letting go until she was damn well ready.

They collapsed against each other and lay without moving, trying to get their breath back. Finally, she said, "I don't even remember why I woke up. But thank God I did."

He laughed, and the laugh turned into a groan as she pinched his inner thigh, then started tickling. He barely had the strength to roll away from her. "Christ, you're amazing," he had time to say before falling into a sleep so deep, it was nearly unconsciousness.

# Chapter 7

Kara came awake like a cat in the dark. As always when in a strange place, her waking thoughts were chaotic—Where am I? Is it safe here? How long have I been here? Who's after me? *Am I safe here?*

Memories flooded back and she relaxed, then despised herself for relaxing. She certainly wasn't safe in Jared's bed. For one thing, the man was deluded into thinking he cared about her, but she wasn't falling for *that* one, thanks very much. For another, the man was ridiculously talented in bed, a gold star lover—not that her experience was vast, but still. She thought about his hands on her, his mouth on her, and felt her face getting warm. He'd done things to her no one had ever done, things she'd never even thought of. And her body craved more, needed more.

She forced her mind away from Jared's overall marvelousness and back to the problems at hand.

Carlotti had a contract on the man whose bed she was sharing. Jared was a bomb waiting to go off and blow her life to pieces. It was a simply a matter of what happened first—Carlotti got the drop on them or Jared broke her heart.

*Then run*, her mind whispered treacherously and she squirmed in shame. Jared saw a lot—too much, sometimes—and he was right when he called her a coward. It was her nature to run from adversity and emotional danger. Jared had meant something to her from the beginning and that had only made her fight harder.

Now it was too late. She quit pretending when he coaxed her into staying overnight. She was in love. She was such a stupid fool she had given her heart to someone again, despite life's cold lessons—and look who she'd picked to fall for! A doctor who was as straight and narrow as a ruler, whose idea of big trouble was running out of gauze pads.

Lying next to Jared's comforting warmth, she wryly reflected on the fact that she would take murderous goons and the threat of jail over falling in love any day. She was the thief, but Jared had effortlessly lifted her heart and taken it for himself. His sleight of hand had been so superb, she had never seen it coming.

She sat up and looked around his bedroom. There was plenty of light from the moon and she observed a single man's clutter, a man who worked long hours and cared little for keeping up with the laundry. Despite the mess, his bedroom was comfortable and inviting. And big. Plenty of room for two.

She shook her head at her foolishness. Jared was beyond marvelous, with a healer's comforting touch and a comedian's wit, but he would eventually leave her, as everyone did. It wasn't a bad thing, it was just the nature of things, of men, of family. She knew once you grew to depend on someone, they would immediately leave you to an orphanage or the streets.

Worst of all were the foster families, the ones who didn't have to care for you, who were paid by the state to feed you, but then pretended they *did* care, right before they shipped you back to the state home. She had sworn by the age of ten never again to fall into the trap of caring and for the most part had kept that promise to herself. There had been a few slips, of course, but the lesson, hard learned, sometimes had to be reinforced.

She eased from the bed and Jared never stirred, though he muttered unhappily in his sleep and his hand sought her. She tucked the blankets beneath his chin, marveling at how boyish and charming he appeared even in sleep. She hated to leave him, this warm, comfortable room, this place. And because she hated it so much, she made herself get dressed and get the hell out.

Once on the street, she paused for a moment, observing the predawn traffic and wondering what to do now. Her attitude toward Carlotti had always been reactive, not proactive—she never went looking for trouble, but when it found her she defended herself. That, she belatedly realized, was not the way to handle the Carlotti situation. The more time she spent with Jared, the more foolish her thoughts became.

She couldn't quit bodyguarding, couldn't walk out of Jared's life and leave him on his own until the situation resolved itself. Good doctor Jared shortly would become a mob prisoner, then a cadaver. So how best to complete her service and get out of Jared's life?

Proactive, she reminded herself, buttoning her jacket against the early morning chill. Find Carlotti. It wouldn't be difficult. Find him and kill him. Now. Before one more day went by. And then get out of Jared's life—*Before he hurts you*—while there was still time. She had never killed anyone— that sort of thing was never necessary during her hacks—but she figured Carlotti was an excellent place to start. Given a choice between taking an irrevocable step toward corruption and keeping Jared safe—no contest.

Okay. One of Carlotti's girls was living at Meg's pross house. Meg owed her several favors. It was a good place to start.

Kara stepped down from the curb to flag the cab at the end of the block.

"I don't know if he's here for *sure*," the prostitute repeated nervously. The woman's street name was Krystal—"That's with a 'K', sugarbumps.") and while she claimed to be not yet drinking age, Kara

110

put her at mid to late twenties. Of course, Krystal-with-a-K could be right. The street was tough on faces and the average pross had a shelf life slightly longer than yogurt. "And I don't know why we had to come here *now*. I told you, if he *comes*, it won't be 'til *suppertime*."

Krystal slung her purse over one bony hip and glared at Kara. She was a tall woman, underweight and twitchy, with a long, narrow face and a gleaming gaze that watched avidly for disaster. The woman had observed a child slip and fall down hard enough to skin both knees bloody, and had laughed so hard she'd stumbled off the curb. Kara hadn't commented, but did walk over and assist the child to his feet, brushed him off, and sent him on his way. She wasn't surprised, by either the child's misfortune or Krystal's cruelty. The prostitute with a heart of gold was a movie myth. The very nature of their work bred savagery and indifference. Their lives were so hard, who cared about anyone else's? Kara didn't like it, but she could understand it.

"I appreciate you showing me the place," she replied absently. The warehouse was close to the train depot and she imagined it had once been used to store incoming shipments. Krystal told her Carlotti used it to house stolen goods and black market movies—here a customer could get a tape of a movie before it even hit the theaters. "But it's beginning to occur to me that I've been something of an idiot."

"Huh?" Krystal replied, her ratty gaze darting all

over the empty first floor. "What are you talking about?"

It had taken Kara hours to seek out Krystal and talk the woman into giving her directions to the warehouse. Krystal's insistence on accompanying her should have been the first tip-off. Now it was past lunchtime and Kara remembered that, as usual, no one knew where she was, or when she was expected back. She'd been led to an abandoned warehouse by an untrustworthy woman who laughed at a child's pain. And she only had Krystal's word that Carlotti wouldn't be here for another six hours.

*The oldest trick in the book,* Kara thought, shaking her head as she heard the bolt from the front door shoot home, locking them both inside. *And I fell for it. Because I wanted to rush and get this over with so I could run away from Jared. Stupid, stupid girl. Now pay the price for your cowardice.*

A few boxes tumbled to the floor across the room and then Anthony Carlotti was walking toward her, flanked, as always, by several musclemen. *And one musclewoman,* she reminded herself, seeing Krystal's malevolent grin. The woman had not been nervous about betraying Carlotti. She'd been nervous that Kara would smell a trap and vamoose.

"Looka this," Carlotti said, pushing more boxes out of the way, "we got us a thief in the house."

Krystal cackled dutifully, watching avidly while Carlotti slipped black leather gloves over his huge fists. Kara knew he wore them when he planned to beat someone to death. It was a special murder saved for special occasions—rivals, traitors. Hated enemies. Beating someone to death hurt his hands, broke bones, so he didn't do it often.

"Gosh," she said mildly, relishing his annoyance at how she wasn't cowering, "lucky me." She knew her expression was mellow, her tone unworried, but inwardly she was seething at her foolishness; she had stopped making such mistakes by her eleventh birthday. Jared had shaken her in more ways than one, but she couldn't blame him for this. No, she was definitely in a mess of her own making.

And what a mess it was. She could have taken two of the bad guys, maybe three, not counting Carlotti. But there were five total and, judging by the bulges in a few jackets, three of them were armed.

She came to the unsurprising realization that she was going to die, that it was going to take a long time, that they would probably strip her of her valued control before it was over. She didn't mind dying so much—or wouldn't have, before loving Jared—but above all she wanted to die well. And she was pretty sure that wasn't going to be possible.

Worst of all, she had left Jared unprotected. Once she was bleeding her life out on the filthy warehouse floor, Carlotti could pick Jared off at his leisure. All it would take was one phone call—come quick, Dr. Dean, your lady friend is in trouble. And Jared, blessed do-gooder, would come on the run. Dying was awful enough. Dying with the knowledge that she had killed Jared with cowardice was too much to be borne.

While Carlotti edged closer—cautious, even on his own turf, surrounded by his own people—she decided she would have to take Carlotti with her. She could do that much for Jared.

While she pondered how best to kill her killer, Carlotti had crossed the room and slapped her hard enough to slam her back against the table. She shook off the blow, blew her hair out of her face, and asked with mild curiosity, "Do you throw like a girl, too?"

Carlotti reddened and raised a clenched fist. Kara gathered herself for the fight of her life—and his. Time seemed to freeze for a long moment and then there was a brisk knock.

Surprised, they all looked toward the door.

# Chapter 8

"**O**kay, Jared, don't panic." This was good advice, which unfortunately didn't take because he was trying to put his pants on backwards.

Finally dressed, he fled the apartment, cursing himself at every step. He had known when Kara left, of course—he'd been a light sleeper all his life. A mouse couldn't creep out of his bed without him knowing it. He assumed she wanted to get up to have some time to herself, maybe use the bathroom. The click of the front door closing had brought him bolt upright in bed. By the time he'd thrown his clothes on and gotten to the street, she was long gone.

And he knew what she was going to do. He wasn't sure how he had come by the knowledge—no, that was a lie. He knew Kara, had watched her, fought beside her—sort of—had his hands on her while she came, held her in his arms while she slept. He knew her fear, though he only had a vague idea of its depths. And knew the only way someone with her warrior's honor could leave his life was if she eliminated the threat to him.

She had gone after ole One Eyebrow. He had to stop her or, if he was too late to do that, help her. And there was only one person he could turn to for help.

"So what'll it be, doc?" Meg asked, covering her surprise with a friendly leer. "Half and half? Around the world? All my ladies aim to please. Satisfaction guaranteed."

"Don't be ridiculous," he snapped.

"Yeah, you're right," she admitted, "all my girls are retired now. The most we could offer you is a hickey. Five bucks," she added.

"For God's sake! I'm here to find out where Kara went, not to indulge in a business transaction." Jared tried for fierce and hoped like hell he wasn't blushing. His face felt hot, but that could be because he'd run all the way here from his car. "She's gone after ole One Eyebr—Carlotti. I've got to help her."

Meg snorted. "Help her what? Get killed?"

Jared fought the urge to choke the former madam. It was more of the street "Kara doesn't need help and even if she did, you should leave her alone" mentality. Stand alone and never ever ask for help, because that meant you were weak. *These people,* he thought grimly, *have watched too many Clint Eastwood movies.*

Even the street punks he'd backed down had cautioned him to leave Kara alone. Funny, how the street knew her—*their*—business, but wouldn't or couldn't interfere. Scared of Carlotti, or more of that maddening street code? Either way, it was an infuriating impediment.

He'd brought his car to a smoking stop in front of a fire hydrant and all but leapt onto the cracked sidewalk. He'd charged up the stairs to Meg's place, only to find his way blocked by three husky teens, any one of whom would have been a formidable opponent.

He hadn't cared. Clenching his fists, he'd snarled, "Out of the way, boys. I'm a doctor. I can hurt you in ways you can't begin to imagine." Which hadn't impressed them, he was annoyed to note, but one of the boys had recognized him as the man who'd shown up with the Avenging Angel the day before and told the other two to back off.

Jared had strutted past them. "That's right, punks. Touch me and the Angel will have your braces for Christmas tinsel. She worships the ground I walk on, you know."

He had ignored the hoots that greeted this statement. He'd also ignored the parting advice of one—"Stay out of this, homely."

"That's 'homey,'" he'd muttered back, only to hear more laughter.

Now he was faced with Meg, who wasn't any more help than the boys had been. "Don't you understand? She's in this mess because of me. She's taking on Carlotti because of *me*."

"My, aren't you the powerful one. Didn't think anybody could get Angel in a mess without her saying so." She gave Jared a long, pitiless look. "And there's no mess she's in that you won't make worse. You're not one of us, doc. You're a citizen. I bet you even pay taxes."

"Thanks for reminding me, and by the way, it's not a dirty word," he snapped. "And I've had quite enough of the 'you wouldn't understand you're not one of us' bullshit. Just because I didn't grow up around the corner doesn't mean I don't know about trouble."

Meg was silent. They both looked up when the door to the entryway opened and a girl—a kid, no more than thirteen, probably—entered, carrying two glasses of ice water. She handed them to Meg, gave Jared a brief, uninterested, look and left the room.

"Have something to drink," Meg said at last, handing Jared a glass. "You probably need it. Running all over the place like an idiot. You know Kara won't thank you for butting in."

Relief made his knees want to buckle; he willed himself to stand straight. Meg had said Kara wouldn't thank him, which sounded an awful lot like the canny former prostitute had knowledge she was going to share. "*I* won't thank you," he said quietly, "if something happens to her because I'm not there to help. Especially when you know where she is."

"I don't know exactly, I only have a guess. I didn't have time to warn her about Krystal," she said,

118

sounding annoyed, "and that's the only reason I'm telling you anything. If I thought she had the whole story, I wouldn't say shit and there wouldn't be a thing you could do about it, pretty boy."

"Warn her?" he asked sharply. *Definitely don't like the sound of that, oh no.*

"I wasn't here when Krystal left with her. Kara can take care of herself, but Krystal's a snake and snakes bite everybody, even snake handlers."

Mystifying, but interesting. Jared nodded encouragingly.

"I was about a day away from kicking her skinny ass out of here. She was trouble from the start. Not because of what she's been through, what she's done. She's trouble because she likes it. I can't put up with that. Won't."

Well. Any woman a tough cookie like Meg didn't like definitely bore watching. Suddenly realizing how thirsty he was and realizing he wasn't going anywhere until Meg had her say, he drained his water glass and gagged on the lemon slice before spitting it back among the ice cubes.

Meg sighed and he had a moment of sympathy for her. The woman was getting ready to do things that went against everything she had ever learned. She was going to trust a stranger, she was going to help that stranger interfere in street business, and she was as much as admitting the infamous Avenging Angel needed help. Big-time sins, where she and Kara had come from.

He didn't care. Concern for Kara drove out consideration for Meg's moral dilemma. If he had to, he'd throttle the information out of the woman and to hell with anyone who might get in his way.

"I don't know for sure," Meg said at last. "But there's a warehouse Carlotti's been using lately. Krystal was busted there last week, but the cops only hauled her in, nobody else in the gang. You might want to try there. It's down by the waterfront. Third and Lancaster. You can't miss it, it takes up the whole block."

"Good-bye," he said, putting down his glass and turning to leave. Meg reached out, flash-quick, and snagged his elbow. Jared was astonished at the smaller woman's strength. He could have broken her hold, but it would have taken effort, as well as precious time.

"Freeze, Dr. Doofus. Do you have a plan? I mean, besides barging through the front door and getting shot in the face?"

"No. That was pretty much my plan. Let go, will you? You're cutting off the circulation."

"You in the market for some advice, citizen?"

"Absolutely."

"Some of my girls. They get sick a lot. Too many years standing on street corners, you'll catch everything, you know?"

Jared nodded. He did know. Prostitutes were easy prey for just about any bug that came along. Many of them were afflicted with chronic colds, viruses, and the tunnel honeys developed emphysema in a distressingly short time from exposure to car exhaust.

"Well," Meg was saying, "they don't like to go to

the clinic. The wait's long, they have to sit through lectures from people who don't know shit about the life, and if you don't have insurance it's—"

"A nightmare of paperwork and bureaucratic indifference," Jared finished. "How about I make some housecalls for you? Maybe two or three times a month?"

"Dara!" Meg yelled, startling him, and the same girl who had brought their drinks reappeared. She was actually, Jared noticed, much younger than early teens. He didn't want to think about the circumstances that had led her to a home for retired prostitutes. "We still got those boxes left over from last night's supper?"

"In the alley."

"We also need to borrow one of your birthday presents. The one I got you for a joke."

Dara almost smiled. The child reminded him of a younger, more solemn Kara. "Be right back," she said, turning to leave.

"Assuming you don't get killed, doc—which you probably will—I'll expect you here a week from today to give some of the girls a checkup."

"Thanks for the vote of confidence."

"I don't think your presence will make a damn bit of difference," Meg went on ruthlessly, "but you never know. If nothing else, you might make a good distraction. So here's what I suggest you do . . ."

# Chapter 9

There was another knock on the door.

"Who the hell is that?" Carlotti asked, perplexed.

He was right to be perplexed, Kara thought. This wasn't a neighborhood where one knocked. Certainly the police wouldn't bother. And anyone who belonged in this warehouse was here right now. So who was it?

"Girl Scout cookie time already?" she asked brightly.

"Shut the hell up. Joey, go open the door."

Joey did, first freeing his semi-automatic and holding it loosely in his gun hand. Kara noticed he hadn't bothered to ratchet a bullet in the chamber, a fact which cheered her immensely. How nice to know that Carlotti, a monumental idiot, still chose to surround himself with fellow morons. She almost laughed aloud and got ready.

Her mood had dramatically shifted and she wondered at it. And in another half-second she was able to put her finger on the reason for her sudden high spirits. For once in her life, she wasn't acting like a rat in a trap, wasn't wondering how best to scuttle away and live to thieve another day. Now she was thinking like an assassin. It was unsettling, but nice to be thinking about something besides how to run.

Joey unbolted the door and swung it open. It groaned on heavy hinges which cried out for oil, revealing . . .

Jared.

"Pizza?" Joey asked.

Kara closed her eyes. The stress had finally gotten to her. All those years of living by her wits, of cheating death—and various arresting officers— had finally caught up with her; in this moment of extreme peril, she was hallucinating.

"Yeah, that's sixty-nine ninety-five," Jared was saying. Kara opened her eyes. It *was* Jared. Dressed in a red jacket, a red cap, and jeans. Perhaps most surprising, he was carrying six large pizza boxes.

It wasn't an actual delivery uniform, she realized, but the bold colors—coupled with the pizza boxes—tricked the average observer into thinking he was a delivery boy.

"We didn't order no pizzas!" Carlotti shouted. "So get the hell lost!"

"What?" Jared yelled back. "Dude, if you don't pay, it gets taken outta my paycheck!"

"But we didn't—"

"So you're payin'! I gotta pepperoni extra cheese, I gotta meatlover's special, I gotta vegetarian, I gotta sausage onion mushroom, I gotta cheese—"

"But we didn't order any pizza," Joey said, still trying to puzzle this out. Kara could practically read the man's torturous thought process—We should be beating the crap outta the bimbo, instead we're talking about pizza? Wha?

"Sixty-nine ninety-five, man, let's go, I'm double parked." Suddenly, shockingly, he hurled the pizza boxes at the bad guys, who had loosely clustered around Joey, and yelled, "Run, Kara!"

Joey's elbow came up, blocking, but it did no good—the boxes went everywhere, their tops popping open and spilling their load. To her astonishment—and Kara had thought nothing more would surprise her this day—she saw the boxes were filled with dozens and dozens of marbles.

Pandemonium. Joey was the first to fall, hitting the cement floor so hard his gun was jarred from his grip. Jared snatched it from the floor, cat-quick, then pointed it at Carlotti with wildly trembling aim, squinched his eyes shut, again yelled, "Kara, dammit, run!" and pulled the trigger.

Nothing happened, of course; she doubted Jared knew how to pump a cartridge in the chamber. Frankly, she was surprised he'd known which end to point at Carlotti. But it didn't matter; it was his purehearted effort that counted. He'd risked everything to come here, the moron, and had been ready to violate his healer's oath to save her life.

She had no trouble keeping her balance on the treacherous floor; it took stamina and concentration, both of which she had in spades. She was at Jared's side in an instant, pulling the gun from his grip and throwing it as hard as she could. She knew more about guns than her lover—almost anyone would—but she had always concentrated on the martial arts, never feeling the need to bring a gun along on her hacks. Besides, she had noticed before that those who were good with guns often depended on them to the exclusion of everything else.

Three of the goons were scrambling on the floor like dazed crabs. Marbles were still rolling everywhere. One of the thugs had racked his knee as he'd fallen and he was not at all interested in getting up and joining the fray. Instead, he rocked back and forth on the floor, his lips skinned back from his teeth, holding his knee with both hands. Kara heard a click and shoved Jared out of the way just as the air exploded with sound.

"The idiots don't even have silencers," she muttered, flinging a pizza box at another bad guy's head. During his flinch she kicked his legs out from under him and yanked the gun away hard enough to break two of his fingers. The small crackling sounds—and the significantly louder scream of the creep who'd actually *shot* at *Jared*—were infinitely satisfying. For a moment, she was sorely tempted to empty the clip into the goon's head and almost smiled—she hadn't been nearly so furious at the danger to her own life.

Joey had gotten to his knees, only to topple over as Jared dealt him a vicious kick to the kidneys.

Kara broke a chair over another one, kicking his gun across the floor, where it skittered beneath a table. She looked around, grinning and unable to stop. Chaos reigned. In less than thirty seconds, the situation had radically changed. Now it was no longer a question of "Gee, I hope I can kill Carlotti before he kills me". Now there was no doubt. She would kill him and end this. There was time to do one of two things—save herself, or do what should have been done years ago.

No contest.

She started toward Carlotti, who was trying to help two of his men up at the same time, urging them to "get her, shoot her, fuckin' get her, dammit!" too much a coward to take her on alone. He wasn't armed—he'd been planning to beat her to death—and she was still grinning, could feel the expression on her face and knew it wasn't a nice smile, but oh, she wanted his death so badly, wanted Jared safe forever and now, now it was going to be done, it finally—

Someone tackled her from behind; it was like being taken down by a diesel truck. She got her arm up in front of her face before her nose connected with the cement floor, then felt herself lifted quickly and hustled toward the door at the back of the room. She got a whiff of Jared's aftershave and in a moment of perfect understanding realized what he had done. And what he had prevented her from doing.

"Jared, let *go*! I can't let the opportunity go by, I can't run away from this! You idiot, you're ruining everything!"

"Wrong, blondie," he said, and the tricky bastard didn't even sound out of breath. He had one of her arms twisted into the center of her back and was propelling her so firmly and quickly, it was all she could do to keep her feet.

They left the chaos of the main room behind them and, to the stunned mobsters, it must have seemed that they disappeared into the shadows.

# Chapter 10

"**Y**ou idiot!" she hissed as he yanked her into a small storage room. She got a brief glimpse of a short counter, some mops, and a few pails before he closed the door. She stood perfectly still, waiting for her eyes to adjust to the dark while he stumbled around, feeling for something to block the door. "You—you might have been killed!" Never had she felt so many conflicting emotions—anger, relief, giddiness, fear. "I left you in bed for a reason, you know. I—"

He shushed her scolding with a long kiss, then lifted her and placed her on the counter. She wondered how he could see a thing in the dark and was a little annoyed, frankly. *She* was the fly-by-night cat burglar, for heaven's sake—it was ridiculous that she had been cursed with lousy night vision.

She pulled away from the kiss—not without regret—and opened her mouth to continue listing his wrongdoings, and brother, they were legion, when he pinched her on the underside of her right breast, hard.

"Ow!"

"Quiet. You don't get to yell at me. I get to yell at you. Quit putting yourself in danger for my sake!"

"Keep your voice down." They had been whispering and it was doubtful Carlotti and Co. had mobilized yet, but old cautionary habits died hard.

He sighed, a depressing sound in the dark. She wished she could see his expression. "Look, Kara, I guess I'm a—a closet chauvinist."

"Closet imbecile, you mean."

"I know you can take care of yourself most of the time—"

"*Most* of the time?"

He ignored the interruption. "But I can't help coming to your rescue. And admit it! This time you needed it. If I hadn't distracted those guys, you'd . . ."

She didn't want to think of that. Her stupidity. How she had been led to the warehouse like a child of five. "You should have stayed home," she said stonily.

"You're not listening. If you ever leave me alone in the dark to go off and confront a killer—if you ever try to take on five men by yourself again, *I'll* break your neck." He was hissing in her ear, making all the hairs on her left arm stand up. She couldn't tell if he was scolding her out of relief or if he was really furious. "I'll take you to the D.A. myself. I'll never cook lunch for you again. And . . . and . . ." Then he kissed her again, hard enough to make her lean backward. It was a bruising, possessive kiss and she could feel her unwitting response to it, feel the wanting flare up in her like newspaper catching fire.

"We have to get out of here," she managed, and he took advantage of her open mouth; his tongue thrust past her teeth and she gasped. "Carlotti—"

"Could you not say another man's name when I'm having my way with you?" he teased. His anger seemed to have vanished for the moment and she was glad. She didn't like being reminded about leaving him alone. She had regretted it the moment it was done.

"We're still in a lot of trouble," she couldn't help reminding him, feeling like a nag but unable to help it. "Carlotti and his men will tear this warehouse apart looking for us. We have to be absolutely quiet—"

"You're right."

"—and find a way out of here without being seen."

"This warehouse takes up the block," he pointed out. "They'll be searching for a while."

She assumed he was intimidated at the thought of leaving the temporary safety of the closet and took pity on him. He had been remarkably fearless when he posed as the pizza delivery man, but Jared was a regular guy and not used to the violence that was her day-to-day existence. And he did save her life. Probably. The least she could do was humor him before pushing for them to leave.

"Remember," he whispered, so quietly it was

more breath than sound, "no noise." Then he stood very close, so close he forced her knees apart. Not for the first time, she vowed to never again wear a skirt, even a borrowed one, but she'd thought a skirt would fool Carlotti into seeing her as more helpless than she really was.

Jared's fingers were sliding up her inner thighs.

"Wha—"

"You have to be utterly silent," he murmured in her ear, so quietly she had to concentrate carefully to catch what he was saying. And concentrating was difficult, given where his fingers were. "If you make a lot of noise, the bad guys will find us, and what kind of a bodyguard would endanger the man she's supposed to protect?"

Shocked beyond words, she realized the depth of the trap he had set for her. She couldn't protest much louder than a whisper—which he could ignore—and couldn't fight him off, however carefully, without bringing attention to their position. Anything much above a whisper could be heard, and what if Carlotti's men were in this hallway right now? They most likely were not, but she dared not take the chance. As Jared said, what kind of a bodyguard would she be if she brought the bad guys down on them?

She was amazed at his ruthlessness, at how he was taking advantage of her protective nature to do as he liked, regardless of her feelings.

While this went through her mind, his hands were at her sweater, unbuttoning it and then spreading it apart. Annoyed and strangely excited, and more annoyed at being excited, she tried to slap her knees together, but they merely thudded against his hips. She felt him ease her breasts from their bra cups, then felt his breath a moment before his mouth closed over one nipple. She swallowed her gasp as he sucked hard, drawing her nipple against the roof of his mouth and then tracing a circle around it with his tongue. Abruptly her breasts felt warmer, heavier, and she had the absurd thought that she was wearing too many clothes. And so was he.

He lavished attention on her breasts while she fought the urge to squirm against him. This was beyond madness. This was asking to get caught and killed. This was . . . this was unprofessional! Her distracted mind seized on the perfect description of their situation, desperate to think about something besides his mouth and hands. If she couldn't talk him out of it—she couldn't talk at all—or fend him off with a few well-placed smacks, she certainly wasn't going to let him know how his touch affected her. He would get tired of the game soon . . .

His thumbs were stroking her inner thighs, only centimeters away from the elastic of her panties. And his mouth was still on her breasts, kissing and licking and sucking. Now she did squirm, having no more control of the motion than she did her heartbeat. His touch was so feather light it was almost like a dream. And with every stroke he got nearer her panties, the crotch of which had become embarrassingly damp.

133

When his thumbs slipped past the elastic and caressed her plump outer lips, her hands snapped into fists and she managed to restrain herself from seizing his hair and demanding he *do* something, right now! In seconds, she had gone from annoyance to pure sexual heat. Carlotti could have been standing at Jared's shoulder and she wouldn't have cared. She forgot about the foolishness of Jared's actions and turned her formidable concentration to keeping quiet.

Abruptly, shockingly, Jared spread her apart, a thumb on each fold, and did nothing more down there, just held her apart while kissing her deeply, sucking her lower lip into his mouth. Her knees slapped into his hips again as she wriggled against him, trying to get closer, to touch more of him, but he stayed where he was, taking her frustrated whimpers into his mouth and nipping her gently as a warning to stay quiet.

He breathed a command into her ear and she complied at once, hooking her legs around his waist. He lifted her with one arm, and with the other hand stripped her panties past her hips, setting her down and pulling them off as she let go of his waist. He slowly inched her skirt past her thighs until it was bunched around her waist, then passed his hand down her lower stomach, pausing to caress the forest of hair above her aching center. Everything was aching; her breasts wanted his hands back, her nipples were so tight and hard it was almost painful, and as for the sensations below her waist . . . She bit her lip, hard, so as not to shriek at him to take her now, yes, right now, *stop torturing me and take me right now!*

She heard a muffled double thud and realized he had dropped to his knees. He spread her apart again and she felt his mouth at her center. Quick as a thought, she jammed her palm into her mouth and muffled the wild groan she couldn't lock back. Then she hung onto the counter for dear life as his tongue slipped inside her, then retreated and swept across her clit, which had begun to throb in delighted abandon.

She felt a finger push slowly, gently inside her as his mouth settled over her clit and he began to suck, occasionally flicking the trembling bud with his tongue as she swallowed a sob of purest frustration. She had assumed quickies were just that—quick—not drawn-out torture, not being touched with skill and love but unable to touch back, not being able to talk, to beg, to plead. She wanted to pull him inside her. She wanted to jump off the counter and get down on her hands and knees, flip her skirt up over her back and beg him to take her from behind. She wanted to take him inside her mouth. She wanted to touch every inch of him, she wanted to own his body as he owned hers, she wanted . . .

His fingers were gone, his hands were on her thighs, spreading them as far apart as they would go. Now his tongue was inside her again, darting in controlled jabs. She cupped her own breasts, squeezed. Her head fell back against the wall and she stared blindly at the ceiling. She could feel his hands on her thighs, his tongue inside her, darting, flicking, probing. Then he was kissing her clit and she was biting her lips bloody so as not to scream.

She could feel her orgasm like a flower felt the sun start to rise and welcomed it. But mere seconds from the point of no return, Jared abruptly pulled back, leaving her teetering, and only years of hiding her feelings kept her from bursting into frustrated tears. He sat back on his heels and blew, just puffed soft breaths at her swollen, hot, tender flesh, and when he seemed sure she wasn't going to spin away from him into release, he started all over again—his sweet, talented mouth busy between her thighs, bringing her to the edge and leaving her there too many times to count. She couldn't think of protesting, of fighting it, could only hang onto the counter with her eyes closed and her mouth open while he played her body like a virtuoso handled a violin, with skill, with love, with absolute control.

A thousand years later, he stood up and she heard the most welcome sound in the world—he was unbuckling his belt, pulling his zipper down, and who would have thought the simple rasp of metal teeth would bring another surge of heat between her legs? Her eyes had adjusted as much as they would to the dark and he was nothing but a large shadow in front of her, now leaning forward and giving her his mouth. She sucked greedily at his lips, his tongue, tasting him, tasting herself. He broke the kiss and she heard how his breathing had roughened in the dark until he was nearly panting, and wondered if his silence wasn't so much out of safety, but because he could no longer speak.

She felt the tip of him nudge between her swollen nether lips without entering, and even though she didn't have nearly as much of him as she liked, she could still feel him throbbing furiously. She tried to scoot forward, to impale herself on him, but he instantly moved back. She got the message at once and quit trying, grinding her teeth because even now, even now he would not relinquish his dominance, and *ohhhh*, when she was herself again she was going to make him pay for this.

He stroked his thick tip up and down her slick flesh, never quite dipping inside, soaking himself with her wetness. His other hand was squeezing her breast, hard, pulling at her swollen nipple, running the straining peak through his fingers. She gloried in his rough touch, it was exactly what she needed, craved, to offset the delirious madness he'd brought to life within her. Then she felt him slip into her. She had time to think, *oh thank Christ, I'm going to come at last*—before she realized he'd only slid in an inch and stopped.

Her legs started to come up around his waist, she was done with waiting, done with the endless torture, when his hands slapped against the insides of her knees and he held her legs apart. He began to rock, shallow strokes that only brought a fraction of his length within her and then out again, and she sobbed, she couldn't hold it back, but wept as quietly as she could. He sighed. She knew her control troubled him, knew he longed for her to let go with him—was that why he had done this? To make her lose herself? Did he need proof that under her cool exterior she was a hot-blooded woman with very basic needs, needs he was so excellently equipped to meet?

In response to her sigh, her soft sobs, his strokes had lengthened; they were long and deep, and he let go of her legs so she could cling to his waist. His hands slid beneath her buttocks and he pulled her tightly against him, so her exposed breasts were pressed against his sweat-damp shirt, and he pumped, pumped, pumped, done with his teasing touch, now just taking her as she had longed to be taken, in long slick strokes.

"It's all right," he managed softly, his voice so low and thick she could barely understand him. "I'm going to let you come now. And you want to, don't you, sweetheart?"

She didn't answer; she didn't have to. Everything clenched within her and suddenly her orgasm was bursting through her, so hard and fast she buried her face against his shoulder and bit back the shriek of relief and ecstasy. She could actually feel her uterus contracting, feel the throbbing as blood rushed to the very center of her. No sooner had her long-awaited orgasm ended than another began, swooping through her. She was on a roller coaster of pleasure, cresting one hill only to plunge down another, and she could feel him trembling, heard his breathing stop for a moment, and then he was pulsing within her, his grip on her like iron, his face buried in her hair.

A long moment passed while their breathing slowed, while they came back to the planet. She felt him kiss her ear and then whisper, "Never, never, never leave me to wake up alone and afraid for you." And then, more softly still, "I love you."

She wept, and tried to whisper the words he wanted to hear, words she never thought she would say—or feel—but he seemed to understand and shushed her and held her for a long time.

# Chapter 11

"I'm still mad at you," Jared whispered cheerfully, "but right now I'm so relaxed, it's hard to care."

Kara snorted. She was fairly annoyed herself, but couldn't figure out if it was because her pride was wounded at how he so ruthlessly mastered her, or because he'd cheated her out of killing Carlotti, or because he'd come to the warehouse in the first place. But his seed was trickling between her thighs and, as he said, it was difficult to stay angry. What she wanted to do was check into a hotel and spend the rest of the day making love. Instead, she was tromping through a warehouse with her wiseass lover, keeping an ear cocked for pursuit and wondering what the hell to do now.

She couldn't hear sounds of pursuit, which was comforting, but if she couldn't kill Carlotti, it was past time to be gone. If she were alone, she wouldn't worry a jot about silently slipping out of the warehouse unseen. But Jared was at her side and "stealthy" wasn't exactly the best word to describe him.

The "clang" as he tripped over a pail brought this point home, and she swallowed a sigh. Looking sheepish, Jared regained his balance and picked up the pail, apparently meaning to carry it with him.

"When we get out of here," she said at last, "you should go to the D.A. Tell him everything you've seen and ask for police protection."

"Screw that," was the rude reply. "If I leave you alone for a minute, I'll never see you again. You weren't going to come back, were you? You were going to ice the bad guy and disappear on me." His voice was the muted thunder of anger. His eyes told a different story.

"Jared . . . Jared, I'll only get you killed." She swallowed the lump in her throat. "I couldn't bear that. Anything but that."

His gaze still reproached her. "Oh. Okay. But you putting yourself in danger on my behalf, *I* can choke *that* down, no problem."

"Shhhhh."

"Shhhh yourself," he grumbled.

She held up a hand to forestall further arguing and poked her head around the corner. She never peeked. Slow movement gave the bad guys something to train their gun sights on. A quick glance, flash, and gone. "Hallway's clear, let's—"

His hand closed around her bicep, circling it easily, and he pulled her back. She was surprised again at the strength in that hand, then reminded herself that Jared Dean was many things, but he wasn't a wimp. "Listen up, blondie," he said, not unkindly. "I'm not going anywhere. I mean right this second and in general. I know you don't believe me and that's okay—for now. I don't expect you to take me on faith. I know I have to prove myself. I—"

"We don't have time for this," she said with deliberate cruelty, because they didn't, and because she wanted him out of that warehouse and safe and didn't want to hear him explain why it was all right not to trust him. Because if he kept up this . . . this nobility stuff, she'd probably have to break down in tears and beg his forgiveness and never, never, never leave his side. And of course that—all of that—was impossible.

"*Make* time, dammit. I know where you came from. Well, where I come from, it's the worst kind of cowardice to leave a woman—particularly a woman you love—in order to save yourself. It's not gonna happen. I'm never going to the D.A., I'm never going to stay out of the way when you kick ass on the bad guys, and I'm not hiding in the goddamned bedroom while you kill the guy who wants to kill me. Get. Used. To. It."

She looked at him thoughtfully. He wasn't angry—well, he was a little, but that wasn't hot rage talking. He really was a chauvinist, and she should have been annoyed at his ludicrous attempt to repress her, but the reality was, she thought it was kind of nice. If incredibly misguided.

Jared, she knew, never said anything he didn't mean. He was stuck to her like a lamprey, whether she liked it or not. And frankly, the only reason she didn't like it was because of the danger it represented to him. So the question was . . .

"I know that look," he said warningly, "and you can just forget it."

. . . should she knock him out and more or less drag him to the police station? It might be the only way to protect him from his chivalrous instincts.

He was backing up. "Touch me and I'll scream."

She sighed. "Never mind." Once he woke up, he would never remain in police protection. The big idiot would probably take to the streets, looking for her. He'd never find her unless she wanted to be found, but he'd get himself mugged and knifed and any other manner of assault on his person while he blundered about, looking for her.

Kara, checking the next hallway, suddenly realized what she had been thinking. *Not that Jared would leave me,* she thought with dawning excitement, *but that he would look for me! Is that a true perception of his character—of his love? Or am I still foggy from lust? It's entirely possible, the man is ridiculously good in bed . . .*

Further pondering was interrupted by the *click-click* of high heels on tile. Behind her, Jared halted obediently, hefting the pail in readiness. She shook her head at him. She knew that walk. And it answered the question . . .

"Hey!"

. . . what had happened to Krystal during the fight?

"What're you guys doing here?" Krystal, who had rounded the corner, was now staring at the two of them. Her face was bloodless, scared, and she had obviously been crying, but Kara couldn't summon any pity for the woman.

"Running from your boyfriend," Kara said sweetly. Jared glanced at her and raised an eyebrow at the tone he had never heard from her before. "I guess things didn't work out exactly as you planned."

"I didn't—I—he *made* me!"

"Does he *make* you wear those tacky shoes, too?"

"Catfight!" Jared said cheerfully.

"I wondered what happened to you," Kara continued. "You ran, didn't you? Ran as soon as it looked like things weren't going Carlotti's way. Not only did you align yourself with unregenerate scum, you can't even be loyal. Now . . . what? You're lost? Trying to find him? Or us?"

Krystal grinned suddenly, looking not unlike a great white shark. Crocodile tears shone like cubic zirconium on her cheeks while she inflated her lungs for a yell that would, no doubt, bring the bad guys crashing down on them.

Jared moved before Kara could; he grabbed Krystal around the shoulders with one hand and clapped the other over her mouth.

"I wouldn't," Kara warned.

"Ouch, dammit! God, she's got a bite like a hyena. Now what?" he complained, just before his breath whooshed out as Krystal simultaneously buried an elbow in his stomach and brought her spike heel down on his instep.

"Well, hit her back," Kara said impatiently, checking the hall to make sure their scuffling hadn't been overheard. She was annoyed at Jared's interference; this was taking too long and making too much noise. "Shut her up somehow. We can't drag her with us and we can't leave her here."

"I can't!"

"What, can't? You're a doctor, you probably know all sorts of dirty tricks."

"But . . ." Jared trailed off as he tried to hold the wildly flailing Krystal, whose wrathful mumblings through his palm were getting louder, like the hum of hornets in a disturbed nest. "But she's a girl!"

"Oh, for God's sake," Kara said, honestly irritated, but she had to fight a smile. He really was adorable. And Krystal, she was sure, was never a girl. The woman had been born a wolverine. "Then let her go."

Jared dodged a wildly flailing elbow and tightened his grip enough to make Krystal gasp. "Ah . . . sorry. Okay, ma'am, I'm going to let you go, but you have to promise to be quiet. Do you promise?"

Krystal quit struggling and nodded, her eyes slits of rage; Jared let go of her. Krystal's hand shot toward her purse, but before she could finish working the clasp, Kara pivoted on her right leg, swung around, and clipped Krystal on the chin with her left foot. Hard.

Krystal dropped like a bag of dirt. Her purse hit the floor, the clasp popped open, and a butterfly knife slid out, all steel and lethal edges.

Jared looked at the unconscious woman, then at the knife, then at Kara. He shrugged, and she could swear he was embarrassed. "Sorry. I just couldn't do it."

"I know. 'But . . . but . . . she's a girl!'" Kara shook her head and tried not to laugh. "Leave her here. She can't screw us over if she's down for the count."

"Look at this," he complained, holding out his hand. Krystal had broken the skin with her bite. "It'll have to be disinfected."

"And you might consider a rabies booster. Hell, you might want to just cut the whole thing off, play it safe."

"Har, har," he said sourly. "You realize, when we're married, I'm not going to be too cool on continuing your idea of a social life."

She said nothing. Married? Impossible.

"*Niiiiiice* spin kick, by the way," he continued, unaware—or pretending to be—of her sudden discomfort. "It happened so fast, I didn't even see it coming until it was done."

"Thanks. That's the idea."

"It's so nice to have a man around," he sighed, and slung an arm across her shoulders. They continued down the hall.

They surprised two more of Carlotti's goons on the way out. When Kara heard their footsteps around the corner, she was overjoyed. One way or another, she knew, this would soon be over.

The fight—well, Kara's part of the fight—was finished almost before it had a chance to get started. Even though the men were looking for them, they still seemed surprised to actually find Kara and Jared, and she was on them before they'd had a chance to so much as twitch their gun hands. She grabbed the one nearest her, wondering—CLANG!—what the hell that noise was, but too focused—CLANG!—on the task at hand to give it her full attention. She wrenched the man's gun away so hard she heard his wrist snap— CLANG!—then buried her foot in his balls and, when he bent forward in agony, brought her knee up into his nose, breaking it and putting him out.

CLANG!

She popped the clip and ejected the shell out of the chamber, then slipped the rounds out and tossed the now empty clip over her shoulder. She turned, and what she saw so astounded her, she could only stare, the gun falling from her nerveless fingers.

Jared, her gentle healer lover, was attacking the other goon with grim ferocity. With the pail. The man had both arms up to protect his face; his gun had fallen to the floor. Unfortunately, this wasn't the movies and it was taking several blows to knock the man out, and the poor guy kept yelping and trying to fend off Jared.

She was about to lend an apparently much needed hand when Jared stepped forward and swung the pail in a powerful uppercut that caught the man on the chin and threw him back against the wall. He bounced off and hit the floor, flopping over like a fish and then not moving.

Jared dropped the pail—CLANG!—and rushed to the man who had been sent to kill him. His skilled fingers found a pulse, then checked the man's pupils and felt the back of his head. "I don't think I fractured anything," he said, unable to keep the relief out of his voice. "But he'll have one hell of a headache when he wakes up." Then, as if fearing he sounded too much like a citizen, he added coolly, "Teach these guys to mess with us. Where's the other one? You want me to take care of him, too?"

"No, Jared," Kara said gravely. "I managed on my own. Nice work."

She should have told him but couldn't. Absolutely did *not* have the heart to tell him that he'd just bashed an undercover cop into sludgy semiconsciousness.

As a child, Kara hadn't just studied the bad guys to survive. Her other opponents—less deadly, but better organized—were the police and Kara had learned to spot a rookie before he or she spotted her. There were so many giveaways, Kara wondered why the cops themselves didn't catch on.

The haircut, for one—trimmed exactly three quarters of an inch around the collar and perfectly straight. Even when they suffered their hair to grow long and forewent bathing in order to look like street people, cops had trouble pulling it off. How many street people had perfect teeth? How many of the female homeless had waxed legs and shaved armpits?

Their nice, even, three-foot police academy strides were another tip-off. She'd heard the man coming down the hall and had known at once that Carlotti's gang had been infiltrated. And had rejoiced.

That was before Jared had assaulted the man, of course. Now he wasn't just Carlotti's intended victim, he was accomplice to the Avenging Angel and had just committed assault and battery against an undercover cop.

Kara realized it was time for a new plan. There was only one problem. Jared was absolutely going to hate it.

*The real irony,* she thought, still listening for the sounds of approach, *is that I'm going to be busted for assaulting a police officer, when I never touched one in my life.*

She almost laughed.

# Chapter 12

Suddenly, weirdly, Kara was in no great rush to leave the warehouse. Jared couldn't figure it out. He was pretty sure she wouldn't mind if he checked the guy she'd taken down—not that he gave a good damn if she *did* object—and aside from a broken nose, the guy would be okay. But she wasn't moving with the same silent urgency she had been before. She was almost . . . strolling. It was like they were an ordinary couple, exploring an abandoned warehouse for fun. Since there was no longer an apparent rush, he was half tempted to ask her if she'd duck into an empty room for another quickie.

Oh boy. He tried to wrench his mind away from the mental image, but in an instant he was back in the closet, feeling her squirm beneath his hands, listening to her soft whimpers as she strained against him, reached for him, held him to her with all her strength. It had been astonishing, outstanding, hideously dangerous, incredibly dumb in ret-rospect—and worth every sweaty second. He'd brave the danger of discovery another hundred times, if only to feel Kara come alive beneath his hands. Her control was a constant irritant and, worse, made him feel like an utter shit, like she didn't trust him enough to be honest about her feelings.

He reminded himself that teaching Kara to trust would take more than a week, and a week was about as long as they'd known each other. *So rein it in, big boy,* he growled at himself, *it's going to take time to get past twenty years of negative reinforcement. Jeez! That's some ego you've got on you, pal.*

He realized suddenly that they hadn't used pro-tection either time. Both times had definitely been in the heat of the moment, but that was no excuse for his carelessness. He knew he was disease free—oh, hell, of course Kara was, too. She was scrupu-lously careful about everything she ever did; she definitely wasn't going to get caught—literally—with her pants down.

That left a possible pregnancy as their only con-cern. And God help him, he fervently hoped she *was* pregnant. He wanted lots of children with Kara. He wanted a built-in entrance to her life, for-ever. If she wouldn't marry him—and she would, eventually, dammit—being the mother of his child was a good start toward lifelong intimacy.

He noticed Kara was looking at him curiously and, he noticed, didn't even glance around the corner before taking them down the hallway. "What are you thinking about? You're uncharacteristically silent."

"I was hoping I'd gotten you pregnant."

She blushed and he almost laughed. She had the oddest—and most refreshing—reactions sometimes. "I don't think so. I'm not—I never—I mean, I haven't had sex in years, so I don't use anything long-term, like the Pill. But it's not the right time of the month for me." A short pause, then she blurted, "Why do you want me to be pregnant?"

He reached out and took her hand. "I think all the time about the kids we'll have," he said simply. "And if you have my baby, that would keep you in my life forever."

Her eyes were huge. "Wouldn't you be afraid of . . . of how I'd raise him? Or her?"

He almost laughed, but saw her expression—she was deadly serious—and choked it back. "Uh, yeah, let's think about the despicable habits you could pass on—honor, integrity, self-defense, championing the weak . . . Yeah, poor little tyke would be a real scumbag with those handicaps."

She didn't say anything, just kept staring at him. Finally she muttered, "You're too good to be true. This has to end before I realize it." Before he could reply—and what a reply it would have been—she added, "In case you were wondering, I'm not—I mean, I don't have any—I'm all, uh . . . "

"Disease free? Me, too," he said cheerfully. Then, hopefully, "Are you absolutely positive you can't be pregnant right now?" She rolled her eyes at him and he sighed. "Then I guess I'd better pick up some condoms on the way home."

"That won't be necessary," she said quietly.

"What won't be necessary?" He tightened his grip on her hand. "I'm not letting you run away from me again and that's final. I'm in your life, blondie, and that's it. If we were in high school I'd give you my class ring. Hell, if you'd let me, I'd pick up an engagement ring on the way home. Or you could break in and steal one . . ."

Then he heard the sirens. And saw that Kara wasn't surprised, was actually leading them back to the main area of the warehouse.

She didn't answer any of his questions, just determinedly tugged him along behind her as she unerringly found her way back to the room where they'd nearly been killed. It would have taken Jared about a week to find that room again, but Kara had them there in five minutes.

And he absolutely could *not* figure out how she'd known the cops were on the way. It explained her sudden relaxation, how she shifted from urgently wanting to leave to urgently wanting to hang around. But it didn't explain why she was bringing them entirely too close to the cops.

"Are you going to make sure they arrest Carlotti?" he whispered, then realized he could have spoken in a normal tone of voice, because she threw open the door and marched right up to the knot of cops clustered around the handcuffed bad guys. "What are you doing?"

"Good evening, officers," she said politely. "Mr. Carlotti has put a contract on Dr. Dean's life. This is Dr. Dean," she added, prying Jared's fingers away from her hand one by one. "I myself can testify to several attempted assaults, and attempted murder."

"What are you *doing*?" Jared practically shrieked.

"Oh-ho," one of the cops said, grinning at Kara.

"What are *you* looking at, flatfoot?" Jared growled.

"Also," Kara continued loudly, "I need to be charged with assaulting a police officer. Your undercover cop is up on the third floor outside the accounting offices. He's mildly concussed. You'll know him because there's a pail right next to him," she added helpfully.

"Undercover . . ." Jared trailed off in horror. The bad guy he'd bashed was a *cop*? Kara had known? And was going to take the heat for it? "But I was the one who—oooof!" He hadn't been fast enough to avoid her elbow to his solar plexus, which effectively robbed him of enough air to speak for the better part of a minute. He bent forward, gasping.

"That's enough of that," another cop said sternly. Kara obediently stepped away from Jared, her hands in the air. "You're saying you have knowledge of a contracted murder? And felonies? And you admit to assaulting—"

"Yes, yes, can we get going, please?" she said impatiently. "Dr. Dean's not going to be out of breath much longer. Oh! I almost forgot. My given name is Kara Jayne Jones, aka Robbing Hood, aka the

Avenging Angel. Just the other night, I hacked into the Freibur Mansion. I can tell you exactly how I did it. Maybe," she continued politely as another police officer deftly cuffed her hands behind her back, "you want to give the D.A. a call when we get to the station house?"

"We'll straighten all that out later, ma'am. I'm going to read you your rights now, okay?"

"It's really not necessary. I have the right to remain silent," she recited obediently, "and if I give up that right, anything I say may be used against me in a court of law. Which is unlikely to ever happen, because the D.A. is so overworked, he'll go for a plea bargain. Also, I have the right to an attorney. If I don't have the funds for one—and I don't, by the way, I give most of my money to charities—the court will appoint one for me. He or she will also be woefully overworked and will push for a plea. Which suits me fine. It's really for the best, Jared. Stop looking at me like that," she added sharply. "I've been selfish to avoid testifying, just because I didn't want to go to jail. You're right, I am a coward. But if I quit trying to hide my past, I can keep you safe, put Carlotti away forever, and stop running." She shrugged and smiled. "It's a no-brainer, really."

He sucked in a breath and straightened painfully. His upper abdomen was throbbing dully. What had she poked him with, a stick of dynamite? "Can't . . ." he wheezed. "Can't let you . . . do this . . . for me."

"Be reasonable," she advised, as a cop, who'd been

156

listening intently while trying not to show it, started to lead her away. "What's a little jail time—okay, a lot of jail time—if it means you're safe?" she continued over one shoulder. "I can do time standing on my head, Jared. It's a lot easier than being out in the real world. Think about it. My rent will never go up!" She shouted that last as the door slammed and he could hear her laughing—laughing!—as she was led to a police car.

"No!" he screamed, lunging after her, only to be caught by the shoulder and hauled back. He turned furiously and threw a punch before he could stop himself. The police officer jerked his head to the side; Jared's fist whistled harmlessly past the cop's ear. The other one pulled a nightstick and smacked Jared in the shoulder with it. Not hard enough to hurt, but hard enough to get his attention.

"Bad idea, my friend," the cop advised softly. "You don't strike us as the average street punk, but even uptown guys know better than to try to clock a cop."

*Not this uptown guy,* Jared thought furiously. *I've already bashed one cop around tonight, boys, don't push your luck.* Then he shouted, "But it's me! It's my fault! I'm the one who—" He struggled to go after Kara again, but both cops locked their arms around him and held him back, with some difficulty.

"We gotta take your statement anyway, sir," the other one said. "You can come down and straighten everything out." His voice was brisk and oddly soothing, a voice trained to calm individuals and control crowds. "And you want to do that, right?"

"I can't let them keep her, put her in a cage . . ."

"Then we better get going, huh? Now, we can arrest you for assault and haul you in that way, or you gonna be a good boy and follow us in your car? You do have a car here, right? Okay. What's it going to be?"

"Trouble," he said shortly. "That's what it's going to be." He shrugged free of their restraining arms and started for the door. "I'll see you boys there."

"You will, of course, obey all city traffic ordinances on the way," the cop said, and his partner laughed.

# Chapter 13

She couldn't even wave good-bye, he thought darkly, pulling into the police station parking lot, thanks to the goddamned handcuffs.

For that matter, he hadn't even known her last name until she'd announced it to the cops. *Announced* it! God!

*She must have been planning this all along,* he thought, stomping up the steps. She had known, somehow, that one of the bad guys was a cop. Let him bash the guy around. Planned to take the heat for it, turn herself in, testify against Carlotti. And his contribution to this plan was to blithely announce he needed to buy condoms. He almost groaned thinking about it.

A police dog, a husky German shepherd, snarled at him on his way to the desk. Jared snarled back and the dog blinked, surprised. A busy night at the 110th precinct, Dr. Jared Dean found himself marching past various drug dealers, pimps, prostitutes, and burglars, all protesting to different police officers, in various tones of voice, that they had been framed.

He stopped before the desk sergeant; miraculously, there was no line. "It was all me!" he proclaimed loudly to the room. "I'm the guy who hit the cop with the pail. I request—no, I *demand* that you arrest me in Kara's place. And let me post bail for her! Right now!"

The desk sergeant, an attractive blonde with eyes almost as pretty as Kara's, eyed him with no change of expression, then said, "Fine, thanks. And you?"

Jared held out his hands, wrists together. "Arrest me! Book me, Danno! I am guilty, I am scum, I am—"

"Guilty scum?"

"But first, how much to bail Kara Jayne Jones out?"

"Have a seat, I'll look into this for you."

"No, you have to arrest me, throw the book at me, handcuff me, lock me—"

"Yes, yes, plenty of time for that. Have. A. Seat."

Cowed—not so much by the woman's tone of voice as her completely unruffled manner—Jared did. He passed the time by spot-diagnosing the many people in the room, as well as fantasizing about all the things he would say to Kara once he had his hands on her. Thirty-five minutes had passed when the desk sergeant crooked a finger at him. Jared was in front of her in three bounds.

"First, no charges have been filed against Ms. Jones."

"What?" Jared could feel his mouth pop open. "But that's imposs—I mean, great! So when are they taking me away?"

"They aren't. Yet." The sergeant—Ristau, the nametag read—gave him a level look and continued. "And a good thing for you, because you can't be arrested yourself *and* post bail for somebody. Officer Carl isn't pressing charges because he really can't. He didn't identify himself to you and your girlfriend as a police officer, you apparently honestly believed he was a danger to you, you were obviously *not* with Carlotti, and the officer in question doesn't even have a concussion."

"But I hit him so many times . . ." Jared heard himself and shut up.

Sergeant Ristau looked smug. "Well, you must be a real lightweight, pal, because they aren't even keeping him overnight for observation. Says he doesn't even have a headache."

In a flash, Jared saw it—it would be much more an embarrassment to the police officer if they *did* file charges, than if not. How to explain how a mild-mannered—usually—physician got the better of a trained officer of the law? Better to ignore it and hope the situation went away.

"So, your ladyfriend is free to go . . . for now."

"Really?" Jared was dazzled. He had no idea the police were so pleasant and flexible. None of the officers he'd run into tonight had even raised

161

their voices, much less tried to slap him around or taken off their pants to show off their butts. It wasn't much like *NYPD Blue*.

Ristau lowered her voice. "Some of the detectives know her—know about her, anyway. And we all heard about the Freibur mansion and how that went down. That bust is going to result in a lot of gold shields. Your friend's a popular girl around here."

"She's my fiancée," he bragged, slinging an elbow against her desk and casually leaning closer. His relief was so great, he felt like swooning. "We're going to have babies."

"That's nice. Anyway, you and Ms. Jones can go, but she's got a meeting at nine-thirty A.M. tomorrow with the district attorney. She gave her 'word of honor' that she'd show and I guess the detectives believe her, because she's free to go. They're gonna finish processing her and you can pick her up. If she doesn't show," Ristau added, gently shoving Jared's elbow off her desk, "a warrant will be issued for her arrest."

*Another warrant, you mean,* he thought, but didn't say aloud. He had trouble believing this was happening—no assault charges and even though the cops *knew* who she was, they were letting her go? He had no idea the real world worked this way. Law enforcement was much more pleasant than medicine.

He thanked Sergeant Ristau, then found his way to Holding to wait while they let Kara go. He was allowed in to where the cells were and wasn't sure what to expect. Scenes from *Chained Heat* and other women-in-cages movies flashed through his mind, beautiful women dominated by handsome guards, lush female prisoners turning to each other for sensual comfort . . . he shook his head. The movies couldn't be completely true.

They weren't. Instead, he saw no more than a half dozen women in the cell with Kara. She was showing a prostitute how to radically extend her pimp's index finger the next time he laid a hand on her. "Bend it *waaaaaaay* back," she was saying, gently demonstrating, "and whenever he moves, or even says something you don't like, bend it back a little further. You can actually walk him where you need him to go. But it'll probably only work once— he'll never let you near his fingers after that."

Three other women were poring over last month's issue of the *Glamour* Do's and Dont's and another one sat by herself in a corner and gazed at Kara with what could only be described as heroine worship. The last woman was sleeping peacefully on the top bunk. Except for the bars, it looked more like a teacher's lounge than a hotbed of hardened female criminals.

Kara heard his footsteps and looked up. Her eyes widened in surprise, which annoyed him. "What did you think?" he snapped by way of greeting. "I was going to let you sit in jail all night?"

"What are you yelling at *me* for?" she protested, rising and coming to stand before him as close as the bars would allow. "And what are you doing here?"

"I'm cracking you out of this pokey." He glared at the janitor, who was quietly sweeping the floor near the door. "And God help *anyone* who gets in my way."

Kara rolled her eyes; the janitor didn't trouble herself to look up.

The tremendous stress of the past few hours caught up with him. "You're in a lot of trouble, Kara Jayne Jones!" he roared in a tone that brought two of Kara's cellmates to their feet. "Turning yourself in, trying to take the heat, having to see the D.A. tomorrow—you just wait until I get you home."

"You sound like my father," she said, exasperated, but she was doing, he saw with surprise, an awful lot of smiling. Shit, was she really that surprised and pleased he'd come? What did she think, he'd have gone gaily back home to eat leftovers and watch PayPerView while she rotted in prison? Well, rotted in Holding? "Somebody's father, I mean," she added. "I don't remember what mine sounded like."

"Kara! Will you focus, for Christ's sake?"

"Her man's comin' down hard," one of the jailed women said to another, not bothering to lower her voice.

He ignored the peanut gallery comment and stuck his finger through the bars, shaking it just under Kara's nose. "We are getting out of here and going home and . . . and then you're in big trouble, a lot of trouble, and you just wait."

"I wouldn't keep my finger in her face, I was you,"

164

another woman advised. She mimed cracking the index finger backward.

"Jared, you're hysterical. Calm down."

"I am not!" he practically shrieked. Then he decided she was right and forced several calming breaths. He didn't say another word to her until they were in his car, on the way back to his place, half an hour later.

"Well!" Kara said brightly. She was, he noticed, more relaxed and cheerful than he had ever seen her. She was staring a lengthy prison term in the face and didn't seem too worried. It was beyond weird. Actually, it was kind of irritating. Didn't she care that she was leaving him? For about thirty years? "It certainly is a relief to be done with hiding. I'm almost looking forward to meeting the D.A. He's been this big boogeyman in my mind so long—Yeek!"

She'd said "Yeek!" because he had abruptly pulled over and slammed on the brakes, bringing them to a smoking, sliding stop.

"You're not," he growled.

"I am."

"You're *not.*"

"Jared. I'll meet with the D.A. tomorrow, who will insist I be held over for the grand jury. And I'll pull some serious jail time for all the hacks."

"But," he said patiently, as if she knew none of this, "you stole from the corrupt, the baby rapers and murderers and drug dealers. And gave the money to the people they victimized."

She smiled sadly. "You're so adorable, you know

that? I'm telling you it doesn't matter. Rules are rules. I'm going down, Jared. For a long, long time. And you're letting me go—."

"The fuck I am." He could hardly recognize his own voice. That low, dangerous tone wasn't at all like him. That wasn't Dr. Dean's bantering tone. That was the voice of a desperate man driven to great lengths to protect the woman he loved.

She ignored him. "—because I won't have you waste your life waiting for visiting day. You'll be old, Jared. Old before your time, old when I get out. I'll be old, too. It won't be allowed."

"You're right about that. Kara, you have to run. I'll drive you to the train station or the bus station or the airport or to Chicago where you can disappear or . . . whatever. You—"

"Jared."

"—can have every penny in my account for tickets. You don't—"

"Jared."

"—deserve jail, not like Carlotti does. All you did was try to stay alive, and dammit, you're not going to jail and that's final!"

"But I am. And that's final. Jared. My darling, my only—" Her voice caught, then firmed, then went rock steady. "I'm done with running. It's like banging your head against the wall—it feels so good when you stop."

"I'll—I'll do something—something really terrible to you if you don't come with me to the airport, right now."

She looked at him and dared to smile. "No," she

said softly, sweetly. "You won't. You love me. You'd never hurt me. Don't you see? That's why this is so hard. You're making it hard. Poor Jared. I warned you. Never say I didn't warn you."

He was silent. She was right. She had tried. She had fought him and their mutual attraction, tried hard to keep it purely business. She had known from the beginning that he meant despair and heartbreak to her and she to him. She had tried to tell him; he'd been too infatuated to listen.

He put the car in gear and pulled back out into traffic.

# Chapter 14

**"I** know that look," she teased. They had entered his apartment, hung up their coats, and Jared had silently fixed Kara a light supper. They were doing dishes now, shoulder to shoulder at the sink. It had been, to put it mildly, a long day.

Jared found it somewhat unbelievable that they were doing something so undramatic and domestic as the dishes. But he had to do something with his hands. He was too emotionally exhausted to think about anything else at this point. "You're thinking about bashing me with a pail," Kara continued, "and hiding me somewhere so I miss my appointment tomorrow."

He coughed and hoped like hell he wasn't blushing. That had been exactly what he was thinking. Trouble was, he'd need something along the lines of an army tank to stop Kara—he supposed he could inject her with a sedative from his bag while she slept, but the chances of doing that and a) not getting his arm broken, and b) maintaining his self-respect, were slim.

"You could never pull it off," she said kindly, as if reading his mind. Sad, really, that she seemed to know him as well as he felt he knew her. Knowledge that should have thrilled them had come too late. "You'd never do it. You're too nice."

He grunted.

"Are you going to spend our last night together sulking?"

"Yes," he growled. Then groaned and shut the water off. "Screw the dishes. Screw *all* of this. I can't believe you won't let me talk you out of going tomorrow. You spend twenty years on the run from authority and pick tonight—*tonight*—to do the right thing? Cripes."

"It's worth the cost," she said quietly.

"Not to me."

There was a long silence while she finished drying the last glass, then she lay the towel on the counter, turned him toward her, and rested her head against his chest. He stood stiffly, not returning her embrace. "I love you for saying that," she said. "I'm sorry about all of this. I should never have gotten you involved."

"Don't say that," he sighed. "I wouldn't have missed it for anything. Wouldn't have missed knowing you for anything."

She laughed and stepped away from him. "God, don't talk like that! You're acting like I'm in my grave. I'm just going to prison for a while."

"A long while."

"Yes."

"Then what?" He threw up his hands, turned his back on her. "What do we do?"

Her hand came to rest on his shoulder and she said softly, more breath than sound, "We make the most of tonight."

He swallowed hard. "Oh, Kara." He turned and pulled her against him, found her mouth, lost himself in her kiss. His lips parted hers, her small tongue curled up to meet his. His body was responding with enthusiasm, but his mind held back. Lovemaking tonight would be agonizing, all the more potent and heartbreaking because it would be their last evening together. He wasn't sure he could do that. Put his heart on a sacrificial altar like that.

Her thoughts seemed to run in the same direction, because she pulled back and looked at him, her eyes mesmerizing pools of deep blue. Her lips were rosy and swollen from his kiss. "Coward," she whispered, and he shuddered and tightened his grip on her.

He swallowed the lump in this throat and abruptly scooped her up. "Saw this in a movie once," he said hoarsely, trying to banter with a voice that wanted to crack. "Always wanted to try it."

"Was it *An Officer and a Gentleman?*"

"*Porky's IV*, actually."

She snorted, then giggled, then laughed outright, which got him started, and by the time they reached his bed, he was staggering and roaring, trying not to drop her, and the tears that rolled down his cheeks were surely from laughter.

He dropped her on the bed and she sat up, reached around, and started tugging at the clip that held her hair up. He stopped her, said, "Let me," and gently freed the large barrette from her hair. The lush blond waves tumbled past her shoulders, almost to her waist. He held the length in his hands, gently combing his fingers through the strands, then brought her hair forward. He slowly pushed her back until she was lying flat on the bed and rubbed her hair, like a coarse silk blanket, over her breasts until her nipples were poking stiffly through the strands.

"No one's . . ." She gulped and tried again. "No one's ever done that before."

"No one's ever loved you before like I do."

"True enough."

"What?" he teased, tickling the underside of her breasts with some of her hair. "No protestations that I don't really love you? That I couldn't possibly love you once I found out who you are and what you've done and—"

She moved like lightning. He felt his wrists seized and he was jerked forward until he sprawled on top of her. "You really have to shut up now," she mock growled, and bit his earlobe.

"Unhand me, you cad!" he shrilled, then kissed her deeply.

Jokes were forgotten as their hands rekindled the desire that was always just below the surface. In a few moments they were both nude, their bodies pressed tightly together.

He pressed wet, hot kisses along the slope of her neck, loving the way his touch made her shiver. "Kara," he breathed, "I'm going to kiss every inch of you."

"Me first," she whispered back and wriggled free of him, then started planting delicate butterfly kisses along his collarbone.

It took forever; it was over in an instant. She didn't just kiss, she licked and nibbled and sucked, her lips caressing every inch of his skin. When he felt her fingers close around him, felt her draw his hot, throbbing length into her mouth, he was certain he was mere moments away from a heart attack. *Let's see,* he thought disjointedly, marveling at how hot her mouth was, how wet, I'll show up in the ER and they'll get some leads on me, then they'll get the defib paddles and shock me, and when that doesn't work they'll crank the volts and shock me . . .

. . . shock me . . .

. . . again . . .

. . . until . . .

"Oh my," Kara said huskily, and kissed the tip of him with no small amount of satisfaction.

"God," he said shakily, throwing his arm across his eyes. "I haven't gotten off that quickly since—"

"Last night?"

"I was going to say since I was a kid," he said frostily, but couldn't help smiling at her as she came up and cuddled against him. He kissed her,

173

tasted himself on her mouth, and at once felt an interested stirring between his legs. "My turn."

He rolled her on her back, cupped her breasts and licked her cleavage, then drew a stiff nipple into his mouth. He could have spent an hour on her breasts alone; their creamy perfection, each topped by a rosy, sweet nipple, seemed to demand his touch. In truth, he ached to touch them, touch her, show her with his body how deeply he cared for her, loved her.

She was sighing in his arms, her fingers were in his hair, she was murmuring nonsense words to him, and when he remembered this was their last night together, that this time tomorrow she would be sleeping in a windowless cage . . .

He shoved the thought away. "Turn over," he said, and when he'd eased her to her hands and knees, started kissing her spine. He trailed kisses all the way down her back, nibbled on a pert, firm buttock, then stretched out on the bed behind her, grasped her thighs, and kissed the entrance to her sex. She moaned and arched, and then he was licking softly, steadily, his tongue cleaving her hot, swollen woman's flesh. He could hear her throaty groans and in response to that primitive sound his engorged cock dug urgently into the bed, and still he licked, licked, licked. He put his hands on her, tilted her hips back and spread her flesh with his thumbs while he forced his tongue inside her. She screamed his name and rocked back against his mouth. He could hear her begging, groaning, and felt like doing a little begging himself, like doing a little *taking* himself and instead let his hungry mouth have free rein. His tongue stabbed at her, his lips tasted her and wanted more of her tangy sweetness, his hands kneaded her firm, white flesh.

"Jared . . ."

He slipped his thumbs inside her, wriggled them. Her flesh was red, swollen, hot, and tasted pretty damned fine. He could have touched her forever. Wanted to. He wished he could see her face, but respected her earlier request, respected her fear at appearing vulnerable, even before him. Maybe especially before him. He loved her, she was coming to love him, and he wouldn't spoil it by forcing an intimacy she wasn't ready for. Not even on their last night together.

"Jared, please . . ."

He rose up behind her and gently took her down to the bed, riding her until they were both on their stomachs. "Please what?" he whispered, smoothing her hair back from her face while fighting the urge to rear back and slam himself into her. Repeatedly.

"Please now," she rasped, "I'll die if you don't come inside me now." She wriggled beneath him and he clutched her shoulders and shuddered all over, knowing if he did what he wanted, what his cock so urgently demanded, they would be done before he was all the way inside. Twice in one night! *Humiliating*, he thought, and could have smiled. "Please, Jared."

"I don't suppose we can renegotiate," he whispered, and tongued her ear. "Are you *suuuuure* you insist on keeping your appointment tomorrow?"

She groaned. "Don't do that."

"I was only kidding," he said, not sure if he was telling the truth. "I—Whoa!" She'd bucked, reared up on her hip, and tumbled him onto his side. They faced each other and she reached for him, her fingers closing around him with care, with love.

"No, you weren't. But I don't blame you." She wriggled closer to him; her eyes were enormous. Her face was flushed, her forehead shining with sweat. She raised her leg and scooted still closer. Unbelieving, he moved to meet her.

He watched her face while he slowly penetrated her. Her eyes widened, her breath caught, her gaze bored into his. If he hadn't come earlier, he surely would have at that exact moment; the intimacy was incredible, like nothing he'd felt before. *Jesus*, he thought, thrusting slowly, mesmerized by her face, *the eyes really are the windows of the soul and hers is . . . so beautiful . . .*

He kissed her softly and she cried out into his mouth, then he felt her tighten around him, felt her press herself as closely as she could. He reached out, found her breasts, stroked her nipples while he thrust against her, and she had barely stopped shuddering from one orgasm when another was on her.

"Oh, Kara," he groaned while she shivered and bucked against him, while her eyes closed and she dug her nails into his back, "I think I'm just about done. I think this is . . . is . . ." Abruptly, shockingly, she jerked away. He was now thrusting into air. "What the *hell?*"

"Serves you right," she gasped, "for trying to use sex to get me to blow off the D.A." Then, incredibly, she shoved her hair off her damp forehead and stuck her tongue out at him. "So *phhhhhbbbtttt!*"

He yowled and grabbed for her. She tussled with him briefly, then let him roll her onto her back and enter her again. Her legs came up, wrapped around his waist, and she thrust back at him, grinning at him the whole time. He didn't know whether to laugh, too, or throttle her.

He came instead, so hard and long he felt his eyes roll back. Then collapsed over her.

"You screamed like a girlie girl when you thought we were done," she whispered into his ear.

"As soon as I get my strength back, I'm going to kick your ass," he growled.

"Sweetie, you couldn't kick a hole through a paper sack." She giggled. "But because you're so good in bed, I think I'll keep you." She stopped laughing, probably remembering she was in no position to keep anybody.

He finally broke the silence. "Let me rest. But only for a little bit. I'm not wasting one minute of tonight sleeping."

"Agreed," she said, and put her head down on his shoulder.


"I had the oddest dream about you," he said, much later. Early morning sunlight was slanting across his bed. Contrary to their best intentions, they had indeed dozed off for a few hours. He had been thrilled to wake up beside her. And nearly cried when he remembered he likely never would again. "The first night you stayed over. Remember? You slept on the couch."

"I remember." How could she forget? "I had a strange dream that night, too."

"In yours, did I dress in an armadillo suit, throw pickles at you, and then hump you like a monkey?"

She shook so hard with laughter she nearly fell off the bed. "No! Don't take this the wrong way, but you're sort of a freak sometimes."

"Says the compulsive thief. What happened in your dream?"

"You raped me, then disappeared."

He looked appalled. "I don't know which idea is worse."

"Well," she teased, "I *did* have an orgasm. So it wasn't all bad."

"Did you now?" His hand closed over her breast. "Let's see if you can have another one. Where were we, er, getting busy? In your dream?"

His palm was rubbing lazily across her nipple, and she was a bit breathless when she replied. "Your couch. You bent me over the arm rest and did as you liked."

"Mmm. Too bad I don't have any condoms. How often can we keep playing baby roulette?"

"Baby?"

"Don't yell, I'm right next to you. Don't you want my baby?"

She couldn't believe they were having this conversation. "Jared, I'm leaving for prison."

He sighed. "Call me a dreamer. I can't help wishing you were ovulating."

"You sure seem to know a lot about it," she said tartly.

He smiled lazily. "Well, I *am* a doctor." His hands were busy between her legs. "Oooh, God, that's nice . . . you're still slippery from last night."

"I was too tired to get up and wash," she said, almost groaned; his fingers—two, then three—dipped inside her with no resistance at all. "And then we . . . we fell asleep."

"Turn over for me." His fingers were busy, busy.

"No fair disappearing when we're done," she said, and was instantly sorry. Why remind him that their time was so desperately short?

"No chance," he said firmly, easing her over on her hands and knees. She felt his fingers, slick from their juices, stretching her, teasing her.

"God, that's nice," she moaned.

"Wait," he panted, and then she felt his engorged tip against her.

"Push hard. Really hard."

"I'll hurt you."

She bit back a laugh. "I want it to hurt. I want to have a sore pussy for a while." *Something to remember you by when I'm by myself in a cell tonight.*

"Kara . . . "

"*Shove.*"

He was reluctant, she knew, but also excited. The word was barely out of her mouth when he obliged with a grunt. And she had been wrong; it didn't hurt. She gasped harshly as he shoved again, his balls slapping against her.

"You're—" She gulped and tried again. "Don't stop."

He thrust, thrust, thrust into her. "Not a chance . . . ah, *Jesus!*"

"Don't stop."

"Thank God." His hands found her breasts, squeezed hard, marked her flesh. His thighs slammed against her. Unlike her dream, she had not the slightest sensation an orgasm was anywhere near. Still, the feel of his cock digging into her, opening her, was strangely exciting. So were his thrusts; they were wild, almost out of control; his arousal was total, it had dominated him completely.

And that was most exciting of all.

"Kara . . . " A strangled groan.

"I love you," she said in reply, and that was it, that finished it for him. He collapsed behind her, breathing harshly. She felt him slip out of her and had time for a quick, amused thought: *Nothing is keeping me from the shower this time.* Then he flipped her over, spread her legs, opened her wide with his thumbs.

His head dipped and she felt his tongue flick across her clit. She squirmed and his mouth followed her. His tongue and lips were delicate, a direct contrast to the pounding he had just given her.

His tongue eased inside her with sweet slowness,

then retreated, then eased back in. She could hear someone whimpering softly and realized she was the one making the sound.

He pulled back a bit and lapped at her, then started licking her the way a child licks a popsicle in July, slowly and enthusiastically. Savoring it. And like a popsicle, she melted.

She brought her legs up and locked her ankles behind his neck. Now he was sucking on her clit, teasing the aching bud with swirls and sweeps of his tongue, and she began to scream. Sort of. In truth she was too tired to scream; what left her throat were shrill, desperate whimpers.

Her hips bucked against his mouth once. Twice. Then she was coming, coming and melting, straining toward him.

They held each other until their breathing slowed.

After a long moment, she said, "We *really* need a shower."

"And a transfusion. Kara, I'm pretty sure you've killed me. I just haven't caught on yet."

She giggled tiredly. "Shall I roll you toward the bathroom?"

"Bathroom later. Snuggle now." So saying, he tucked her head into his shoulder and tossed the sheet over them. "I love you."

She smiled against his flesh. "I love you, too."

# Chapter 15

"You look almost as bad as I feel," he lied. Kara looked beautiful, as usual, but she *did* have dark circles under her eyes. "And I feel like shit."

"You should have stayed home."

"Don't start up with that crap again."

"But you should have," she said, blatantly ignoring his command. "They'll take me away after the meeting and I don't—I don't want you to see that."

"Hello!" he shouted, startling several courthouse staff. Kara was leading them straight to the D.A., like the demented homing pigeon she had turned into. "I saw you clapped in irons and hauled away not even twenty-four hours ago." He looked at his watch. "Not even fifteen hours ago."

"Still," she said stubbornly. "This is no place for you."

"That makes two of us."

In another circumstance, he could have appreciated the grandeur and majesty of the old courthouse. The architecture spoke of a love of design, the mellow wood spoke of a love of caretaking. The building had to be a hundred years old and was magnificent. Unfortunately, right now it was a symbol of everything that was about to go wrong with his life, so he could have gouged holes in the banisters and taken pleasure in it.

"Shouldn't you be bringing a lawyer to this meeting?"

"I waived my right to counsel," she said, not looking at him.

"Cripes! Aren't you taking this throw-the-book-at-me bullshit a little too far?"

She didn't answer him and, disgusted, he quit bugging her.

When they reached the correct floor, there was no one sitting at the secretary's desk, but a man popped out of the small adjoining office and approached them, hand out. "Hi," said the guy who was going to clap his Kara in chains for the next thirty years. "I'm Tom Wechter."

Tom Wechter was the youngest D.A. in the history of the tristate area. The state was proud of him, with good reason. He had an astonishing conviction rate and was boyishly handsome, with dark blond hair cropped short, an athletic frame, a firm handshake. Jared hated him on sight.

He shook their hands. "Why don't we go into my office and have a seat?"

They wordlessly followed him in. He shut the door behind them and the sound reminded Jared of a closing casket.

"Well," Wechter said, sitting behind his desk. His suit jacket was hanging over the back of his desk chair; his sleeves were rolled up, exposing smooth forearms lightly sprinkled with blond hair. His tie was a nightmare—dark green with orange dots. Like a car accident, Jared had trouble looking away from it. "First things first. Dr. Dean, your name is not unknown to me. You made quite an impression on the desk sergeant—Officer Ristau."

"Ah, Officer Ristau," he said fondly, ignoring Kara's raised eyebrow.

"And Ms. Jones, you've also got some fans in the police department. It was suggested to me by several detectives—many who had worked the Freibur case—that I cut you a deal, reduced sentencing in return for your testimony against Anthony Edis Carlotti."

"Edis?" Jared couldn't help asking.

Wechter never blinked. "Family name. However," he continued, "we've had an undercover cop in Carlotti's gang for some time. The officer in question—who had a hell of a headache last night, thanks to you, Ms. Jones—"

Kara moved her foot on top of Jared's and pressed, hard. Jared gritted his teeth and remained silent.

"—has, in the past thirteen months, gathered so much evidence of murder, assault, prostitution, fraud, rape and blackmail—most of it on tape, no less—that Carlotti and his associates have been advised by counsel to plead man one—"

"Manslaughter in the first degree," Kara muttered to Jared.

"Hey, I watch *Law and Order.*"

"—and, it must be said," Wechter-the-robot continued, "Carlotti practically ruptured something agreeing to a plea. So that takes care of him."

"So . . ." Jared hoped he hadn't guessed incorrectly. "You don't need Kara's testimony?"

"No. The better news, Dr. Dean, is because Carlotti has been jailed for reasons that have nothing to do with you, there's no longer a hit on your life."

"Goody," he said dryly. "But Kara is still screwed, right?"

"That's not a legal term I'm familiar with."

Jared stared. The guy was either the biggest stiff in the world, or just dim.

"The Avenging Angel," Wechter said after a short silence. "I've been looking for you for a long time. I've dreamed of getting you in this office."

"I know," Kara said quietly. Her expression was serene, almost bored. Jared swelled with pride. Her life was shattering, imploding, but to look at Kara you might have thought she was waiting for a bus. Or thinking about stealing one. "I've been trying to keep out of your way."

"You've been at this for years, haven't you? The vigilante stuff?"

Kara opened her mouth, but Jared cut her off. "You don't have to answer that, Kara."

"It's a little late to play coy now, Dr. Dean. Haven't you?" he asked Kara.

"Yes."

"How long?"

"How long have I been breaking the law, or how long have I been pulling jobs like the Freibur house?"

"At least fifteen years, I'd say."

Kara nodded.

"Well."

Another silence. Jared was ready to scream from the tension. Not that Wechter or Kara were exhibiting any. That was all right. He was sweating enough for all three of them.

"Well," Wechter said again. "I have a sister."

Kara made a polite noise. Jared considered putting his fist through a wall and bellowing something along the lines of, *Can we just get on with it?*

"Yes," Wechter continued. "She ran into some trouble a few years ago, when she was a freshman in college, when I was the assistant D.A. for this county. She believed a new gentleman friend when he said he was a nice guy, followed him out the back door of the restaurant, went for a walk with him in the park. Ran into three of his friends," Wechter continued coolly, as if reading a weather report.

"They were having a surprise party and she was the guest of honor." He had started tapping his fingers on the desk, the only sign of stress Jared had been able to find in the man. Tap-tap. "So she fought and cried and screamed, and of course no one came to her aid. At first."

Tap-tap. "And about when the first one, the one

187

who'd lured her to the park, was getting ready to take my sister's virginity, someone kicked him in the side of the head hard enough to tumble him off my sister."

Tap-tap. "And when my sister sat up, she saw that not only was her would-be rapist badly hurt, unconscious, but all of his friends were, too. And the only person still standing was a blond girl about her age. Dressed in dark clothing."

Tap-tap. "So this woman—this girl, really—helps my sister to her feet, asks if she needs to go to the ER. My sister says no, thank you. The girl relieves all four men of their wallets. Hands my sister their drivers' licenses. Presses something else into my sister's hand, something cold and hard. The girl wishes my sister a pleasant evening and leaves."

Tap-tap. "And my sister gets all the way home before thinking to look at what's in her hand. It's an enormous diamond ring. Prominently listed, I noticed the next morning, on a police report and worth close to a million dollars. Not that the robbery victim was going to see it again, or any insurance money—he was busy explaining to the vice department why he had so many snuff films in his basement, not to mention the equipment for making same."

Tap-tap. "Isn't that a nice story?"

"I love happy endings," Kara said obediently.

Jared tried to speak, but his mouth was still hanging open. He was trying to process everything he had just heard—Kara had saved this man's sister? *That's* why the D.A. had been pursuing her for so long and so hard? But what did it all mean?

"Luckily I am a man who reveres the honor of his profession above all else," Wechter said with a completely straight face. "Even if the girl in the story had been you, Ms. Jones—and what are the chances?—your past deeds can have no bearing on my duty as an officer of the court."

"What?" Jared practically screamed.

"Of course not," Kara said, with a frown in Jared's direction. "Please allow me to save you some trouble. I will plead guilty to whatever charges you wish to bring."

The D.A. sighed. "Unfortunately, from an administrative standpoint, it's just not feasible."

Jared was having trouble keeping up. "What's not feasible?"

"Prosecution. I don't think I can get a conviction."

"Damn right!"

"Shut *up*, Jared. Mr. Wechter, I've—I'll tell you everything you need to—"

"Who will press charges? The pedophiles? The child pornography merchants? Every house you burgled, every con man you swindled, most of those people are still in prison. But just suppose, for the sake of argument, this office was able to bring charges against you, was able to convince a grand jury that you deserved to be held over for trial. I'm sure Dr. Dean could find someone to say you're unfit for trial."

"Damn right!" Dean said again, louder. This was something he'd never thought of. But hell, his med school roommate was an up-and-coming guy at Bethesda Psych. And hasn't one of his ex-girlfriends just been named chief resident at Beth Israel's psychology department?

"That's . . . very generous," Kara said after a long moment. "But I was arrested last night. My fingerprints were taken, I gave a statement and signed my name to it. It's not that easy to disappear into the cracks."

"Certainly not in a bureaucracy," Wechter said dryly. "Why, we're able to keep track of every little thing around here. Also, your fingerprints didn't take."

"What?" Jared and Kara said in puzzled unison.

"Your fingerprints. We're on a new system now, it's all done by computer. You noticed you didn't get any ink on your fingers? Well, in theory, the fingerprints go right to the computer. Except . . ." Wechter shrugged. "There was a glitch. We can't find your file."

"And the police report?"

"Regrettably, the detectives who took your statement can't find it. They can't even remember your name. Or what you look like. Isn't that the oddest thing, Ms. Smith?"

"Jones."

Wechter shrugged.

Silence, while Kara and Jared digested this. Jared thought—it almost sounded like—it seemed as if the D.A. and detectives were using their influence to let Kara go. But that couldn't be true—this wasn't the movies. Bad things happened to good people. As a doctor, he saw it every day.

"Mr. Wechter," Kara said quietly, "I'm more grateful for these—"

"Bureaucratic foul-ups."

"—than I can say. But it's time for me to face the music, so to speak. I can't keep running. Frankly, I'm glad to be done with it."

"Miss Doe, what purpose is served by putting you in prison?" Wechter asked, equally quietly. "And I might add, this is the only get-out-of-jail-free card you will *ever* get from this office. If in the future you're caught stealing so much as a rice cake, I will prosecute. And," he added with the first smile Jared had seen, "I'll win."

"But . . ."

"Kara," Jared said, turning toward her, "you can't throw yourself on the mercy of the court if the D.A. doesn't have enough to prosecute you." *And clearly doesn't want to prosecute you,* he added silently. "Give it up."

"But . . ." She sounded dazed. She *looked* dazed. About as dazed as he felt, frankly.

"Thanks for stopping by," Wechter said briskly, picking up a pen and pulling a pile of papers toward him. The meeting was clearly over. "It was nice meeting you, Miss Smith."

Kara opened her mouth to correct him. Jared kicked her in the ankle, then grabbed her arm and hauled her up from her chair. "Nice meeting you, too, Mr. Wechter," he said warmly. He could have kissed the man. On the mouth, even! "We'll see ourselves out."

Engrossed in paperwork, Wechter only grunted. He looked up just once, when Jared was ushering Kara out. "Remember," he said, completely deadpan, "crime doesn't pay."

# Chapter 16

"I just can't believe it," Kara said for the fourth time. "I can't believe he let me go. All those years . . . tracking me . . . and I was avoiding him . . . do you think he's worked so hard, risen so fast, so he could be in a position to help me when the time came?"

They were in the same small park where Kara had polished off Carlotti's goons a few days earlier. It was a seedy, disgusting little place, but it was "their" place, so he didn't mind as much as he should have.

He considered her remark. "I hadn't thought about it like that. It's something to consider, huh? It would explain a lot. I mean, the guy's a legend. He never loses a case. He's the most popular D.A. the state's ever known."

"And the handsomest," Kara added demurely.

Jared scowled. "Forget it. You belong to me, sunshine. All he can do is keep you out of jail. I can keep you healthy."

He felt her small hand curl into his, felt her squeeze. "Of course I belong to you. But now what? I spend the last day psyching myself up to lose everything. Now . . ."

"Now you're going to have the life you deserved. Don't you get it? You can do anything you want. No more running. No more being afraid. It's almost like you've been reborn."

"What in the world am I going to do for a living? I never went to college . . . I don't have any societally correct skills. Not that the cops could catch me if I did decide to keep hacking," she added thoughtfully, ignoring Jared's scowl, "but it'd be pretty rotten to reward Wechter's show of good faith by keeping up my old habits."

"Damn straight. Besides, you'll be too busy making a life with me to worry about cracking safes," Jared declared, tightening his grip on her hand. "I want you to marry me."

"Oh, yes," she said casually, "of course we'll get married. As soon as possible, I think."

She giggled at the look on his face. "Christ, that was easy! I figured I'd have to spend the rest of the year talking you into it. Maybe shoot you up with Demerol and haul you before the judge myself."

"*Noooo* . . ." She paused, then slowly continued. "I finally figured it out the night before. And again this morning. You thought—*we* thought—I'd go to jail for years and years. But you stuck by me anyway. You were sure you were going to lose me. But you didn't leave. You . . . you don't leave when things get hard. You risked yourself—needlessly, but it's the thought that counts—for me. You endangered yourself because you didn't want me to get hurt."

"What you're saying," he cut in eagerly, "is in the face of all that, it was pretty goddamned stupid of you to be afraid of making a life with me, right?"

"I hadn't thought of it in quite those terms," she said dryly, "but essentially, yes."

He grabbed her and hugged her fiercely. Her breath exploded against his ear and she wriggled ineffectively. "Please, Jared, I can't breathe," she protested, but she was laughing. "Besides, before you get all excited, I have a request."

"No, you can't knock over Tiffany on our honeymoon."

"Ha ha. I need to use Mr. Wechter one more time—I hope he'll cooperate. Do you think he'll figure I only had one chip with him and I already cashed it in?"

"Kara, sweetie, I don't know what the hell you're talking about. What do you want with Wechter?"

"You'll be approved, no problem, but me . . . I want to join the foster parenting program. From the parenting side, I mean," she added darkly. "I'll give my word about no more hacking, but nobody said I couldn't teach wards of the state how to protect themselves. Nobody said I couldn't teach them that there are houses where nothing bad happens when the shades are drawn."

He smiled sadly. Someday he'd have to ask her

about her entire childhood, beginning to end. He hoped he could hear the entire story without crying—or putting his fist through a wall. "I'm sure Wechter would help you get approved," he said gently.

"You won't mind? The kids will come and go, you know. And they'll be . . . damaged. Some of them. They probably won't like us much."

"Me, probably not. You . . ." He rested a finger on the tip of her nose. "What's not to like?"

# *Epilogue*

Kara sat down at the kitchen table somewhat heavily. At seven months pregnant, getting around was definitely trickier than usual. She'd never been so heavy in her life. So clumsy in her life! It was a good thing she'd given up hacking, because she probably couldn't fit through the front door of a lot of her old targets by now. Slow as she now was, she'd probably trip the alarm a dozen times before so much as touching the front door.

She poured Gary more cereal, knowing he was still hungry and knowing he wouldn't ask for seconds.

It was amazing, she thought, that the great Avenging Angel, scourge of city scum, the feared burglar who could crack any lock and bypass any security system, didn't know her own ovulatory cycle. In the warehouse closet, on Jared's—*their*—living room floor, and in their bed the night before she'd gone to see Thomas Wechter, it had indeed been her time to get pregnant. Two months later, Jared had laughed like a loon when she'd told him, then kissed her on the mouth and immediately taken her to bed. Afterward, he'd charged to Babies "R" Us like a man possessed.

She grinned, remembering, and Gary looked up at her questioningly. "I was thinking about something happy," she explained. "Something about Jared."

Gary nodded and kept eating. He had no comment to add and Kara didn't expect one. Gary was small for his age and his medical records were a nightmare of too many burns and broken bones. He didn't talk much and tensed whenever Jared— or any adult male—entered the room. Kara knew what that meant and ground her teeth in silent rage for what the child had been through.

Jared knew what it meant, too, and did his best not to startle the boy. Since the man tended to bound through their home like a kangaroo on uppers, that wasn't always successful. But in the three weeks Gary had stayed with them, the child seemed to gradually relax, even around her husband.

The boy had stopped eating, she noticed, and was watching her silently. She poured herself another glass of milk and mopped the last of her egg yolk from her plate with a piece of toast. *No wonder I'm so fat I can hardly see my feet,* she thought with an inward chuckle. "Gary? Did you want to ask me something?"

He nodded. "I was wondering . . . how long . . . will I stay here?"

"Well." She considered the answer carefully. "Your stepfather will go to jail. And your mom has to follow some rules to get you back."

"Like stop drinking?"

"Like that and some other stuff. But the thing is, she really, really wants you back. She misses you a lot. She didn't know her husband was doing bad things to you."

"I didn't tell her," Gary whispered.

Kara nodded. "But the way the judge looks at it is, she should have figured it out, you know? That's why you have to stay somewhere else for a while. She's trying awfully hard, Gary, only it'll take time. The judge has to be sure, absolutely sure that you won't be hurt in her house anymore. And it'll take a while for her to follow all the rules so you can live with her again. I would guess you'll be with Jared and me for at least six months." She paused. "Is that okay?"

Gary nodded.

"Because if you would rather stay somewhere else, that's totally okay, and Jared and I won't be mad, I promise. You don't even have to say it to me, you could tell your caseworker—"

"I like it here," Gary said casually, and stood to put his cereal bowl in the sink. Kara was cheered that he'd felt confident enough to interrupt her. She started to get up to put her own plate in the sink when she heard the crash of Gary's cereal bowl hitting the tile.

All the color drained from the boy's face and he cringed away from her. "I'm sorry!" he cried. "I didn't mean to!"

"Hey, Gary, *relaaaaaaaaaax*," she said casually, inwardly wishing the boy's stepfather would stop by just long enough for her to break all his fingers. "I drop stuff all the time. So does Jared."

"You . . . you do?"

"It's no big deal."

He looked as if he didn't believe her. "It's not?"

She raised her plate high, then dropped it. It shattered spectacularly. "Nope. See? Like I said. Happens all the time."

He stared at her. She decided he was still entirely too tense and so dropped, in rapid succession, both their juice glasses and his bread plate.

"Accidents will happen," she said cheerfully as the bread plate broke against the wall. "See, Gary? They're just *things*. You can always buy more *things*."

"Won't . . . won't Dr. Dean be mad?"

"Dr. Dean just wants to know what the heck you two are up to."

Gary jumped again. Jared was standing in the kitchen doorway, looking at the mess and shaking his head.

"Gary had an accident," Kara explained. "Then I had several."

Jared's lips went white as he pressed them together, but the laugh escaped anyway. Kara grinned at the sound and Gary visibly relaxed.

"I'll clean it up," Gary said timidly.

"Freeze," Jared ordered and Gary froze. "You're

both in socks. Gary, I'm going to pick you up and put you in the living room. Kara, I have no idea how I'll heft your gross bulk, but I'll think of something. Then *I'll* clean it up."

"See if you get any tonight," she muttered as Jared gingerly picked his way through the minefield of glass slivers, picked Gary up, and carried him out. Then he returned for her.

"I can do it," she said doubtfully. "I'm pretty coordinated."

He snorted. "Says the woman who tripped getting out of bed this morning. Just stand still." He scooped her up with a theatrical groan, stole a kiss, then staggered into the living room. Gary saw them coming and giggled. He was standing next to their neighbor, Ava.

"Well, hi," Kara said, surprised, as Jared put her down and returned to the kitchen. "I didn't know Jared had brought company. Do you have time for a bite?"

"No," Ava said regretfully. She was a charming matron with two young sons, both of whom had been over to play with Gary. She and Kara had absolutely nothing in common, and Kara didn't know if she liked Ava because of that, or in spite of that. "I just need to call the locksmith. Jack took my keys to work with him and now I'm locked out."

Kara edged toward the door. She had an idea why Jared had brought Ava over. "Did you try the back door?"

"No, but I know it's locked," Ava assured her. "It's always locked."

"Still. It never hurts to try. Let me check it for you. Keep an eye on Gary for me?"

"We broke things," Gary reported solemnly to Ava as Kara left the room.

*Sure,* Kara thought, grabbing her smallest toolkit on her way out, *I promised. No more hacking. But that doesn't mean Ava should be stuck outside for the six hours it'll take a locksmith to get here.*

She grinned. She was hopelessly in love. She had a baby on the way and nice neighbors and was finally part of the system in a good way, a helpful way. She was married to a passionate, amazing, wonderful man and she still got to crack the occasional lock.

Life was good. And, in a way, it was all because of ole One Eyebrow.

Kara laughed and bent to the lock.

# WILD HEARTS

*This story is for my maternal grandfather,*
*John Opitz, who is, as of this writing, at death's door.*
*Again.*

# Author's Note

As with *Thief of Hearts*, *Wild Hearts* isn't a stand-alone book read: single title, 330 manuscript pages, either. It's more of a tidy summary—whatever happened to the D.A.'s kid sister, anyway? Did Kara manage to live the good clean life of a citizen? Did Jared break his neck showing her he too could do a handstand without help? Could the Minneapolis D.A. be the only non-crooked lawyer in the history of practicing law? It's all a fascinating mystery to me, anyway, and one I couldn't leave alone.

So here you go, as Paul Harvey would say: the rest of the story.

# Chapter 1

Kat Wechter stomped out of Old Navy, wondering for the hundredth time why she ever shopped at a store that had such annoying commercials. Not to mention clothes designed for size-two models with no ass and long legs.

*I have an ass,* she thought darkly, *like every woman who eats three meals a day. And as for the long legs? Ha. And again, I say ha.*

At least this time she hadn't wasted an hour of her life she'd never get back, fruitlessly wading through rack after rack of tiny tees and low-slung pants. Cross of Christ! They didn't know the low-slung look was over? Kat had never enjoyed wearing jeans that showed the world her pubic bone, but had endured for the sake of fashion. But she refused, *refused,* to put up with the look when it was so obviously two seasons ago.

Plus, it was laundry day and the only thing at

hand were granny underpants. So ditch the low-slungs, for the sake of all humanity.

She found her car in the Florida parking lot—the Mall of America was so large, the lots weren't divided by letters, but states—and walked up to the driver's side.

To her surprise, there was a man already in the driver's seat. Not knowing quite what to do—scream for help? Haul him out of the car and kick his ass?—she rapped on the window with her knuckles.

He looked at her. She looked at him. Their eyes met. If she hadn't been so pissed, it might have been a romantic moment.

"Boy," he said. "This is awkward."

# Chapter 2

"Get out of my car."

"It's not what you think."

"I think you're stealing my car."

"Okay, it's exactly what you think. But I'm not after a joyride."

"Get out of my car."

"For what it's worth, it's a life and death situation, okay?"

"Get *out!* of my car!"

"Look, you're insured, right?"

"Get out! Of my car!" She fumbled in her purse for her cell phone, mad at herself all over again— why hadn't she noticed him before she'd walked up to the car? She wasn't a total innocent. She knew some men were not, under any circumstances, to be trusted. Ever. *Ever.*

"By the time the cops get here," he pointed out, "I'll be long gone."

"I'm not calling the cops."

"Hey, thanks!"

"I'm calling my brother, the district attorney."

"Awwww, no." The car thief rested his forehead on her—*her!*—steering wheel. "Of all the cars in this lousy giant parking lot, I pick the D.A.'s sister's Mustang?"

"Yeah, so get out now, before you find out what Stillwater State Prison looks like from the inside."

"Honey, I already know." He did something and her engine purred to life.

She slapped the window. "Dammit! Don't you dare!"

"I have to. It's a long story and I don't want to bore you with the gory details. And believe me, sweetie, they're awfully gory. Step back, please," he added politely, "I don't want to run over your toes."

She ran around to the front of the car and jumped on the hood.

He stared at her through the windshield. The part of her mind that wasn't annoyed couldn't help but notice—the man was a stone fox. Auburn hair and big green eyes, true green, the color of crushed peas. Okay, that sounded weird, but they really were a pretty, vivid spring green. And tan, nicely tanned by the wind or the sun, it wasn't a rack tan, and he didn't have the ghostly white complexion of most true redheads. A long nose, reddish brown stubble on his cheeks and chin. Bags under his eyes. Obviously, thieving had been keeping him up nights.

"Please get off the hood," he said, looking helpless.

"My hood."

"Please get off your hood."

"Get out of my car and I will."

"This isn't a *Starsky and Hutch* episode! Come on, get down before you get hurt."

"Get out of my car and I will."

"What are you, playing a recording? Please get off," he pleaded. "I can't peel out of here in a dramatic fashion with you on the hood like a bug about to be squashed."

"Surrender or face the consequences." The hood was uncomfortable and she was clinging to the windshield wipers with both hands. The car needed a wash. "I've mentioned my brother can lock you up for twenty years, right?"

"Yeah, it's come up once or twice."

"So give up now, before someone gets hurt."

His green eyes bulged. "Someone? I'm in here, nice and safe, and you're out there, hanging on like a freak."

"You're a thief!" she yelled back. "And I'm a law-abiding citizen of the state of Minnesota! And you will get out of my car and skulk off into the night like the common criminal you are! Or you will face consequences the likes you have never seen! *Now get out.*"

He leaned over and unlocked the passenger side door. "Get in," he said.

"What?"

"Come on, get down and get in. Then you're in your car, and I'm in your car, and we both get what we want."

Her brain had obviously been left behind at Old Navy—*this is crazy*—because she clambered down—*I must be crazy*—walked around the side of the car—*I know better*—opened the door, and climbed in.

"Don't forget your seatbelt," he reminded her cheerfully, backing out of the slot. "It's the law."

# Chapter 3

"So where can I drop you?" Chess asked, staring at her out of the corner of his eye as the car climbed down the parking ramp.

Her arms were folded across her chest as she stared out the windshield. "You mean where can *I* drop *you*. You're not taking my car."

"Actually," he said apologetically, "I sort of am."

She grabbed his shoulder. "I'm making a citizen's arrest. Citizen's arrest! So you can drive to the police station."

"You can't do that," he pointed out, trying not to giggle. "If you lay your hands on me and rough me up, I could sue you."

"You'd lose. I know a lot of lawyers."

"Yeah, don't remind me," he mumbled. The freaking D.A.'s sister? Of all the lousy luck—she was a stiff, related to a stiff, *and* she was gorgeous. Wild dark brown hair flying all over the place. Black eyes. Not brown. Black. You couldn't tell where her pupils began, which gave her a mesmerizing gaze. Great rack. Great ass. Great everything. She was wearing beat-up blue jeans and a red sweater, and the excitement of the last few minutes had brought a lovely rosy flush to her olive skin.

"In order to make a citizen's arrest," she said, still clutching his shoulder, "I will physically restrain you. Which gets me back to—drive us to the police station. Although the crime took place in Bloomington, I think the one downtown would be better. The address is—"

"I know where the cop shop is."

"Then," she went on like a demented, gorgeous robot with minimal programming, "I will notify the police that I observed a crime. Then I will provide the police with information—you—in order to help them identify the thief—you. Then I'll sign the complaint form. About you. Then I'll go home and have a large steak dinner to celebrate your incarceration. Then I'll appear in court when the district attorney's office asks."

"That's the modern citizen's arrest?" He was horrified, yet fascinated.

"Yes."

"You're assaulting me, you know."

She looked at her hand, which was closed in a fist bunched up in his shirt. She relaxed her fingers and went back to cupping her elbows and staring out the windshield.

"Maybe I could drop you off at your doctor's office," he said helpfully.

"What?" She irritably puffed a dark curl off her

forehead. He tried not to be charmed. He failed. He wondered what her hair felt like—silky, wiry, both? He wondered when he'd stopped thinking about business and started thinking about getting laid.

No, he didn't wonder. He knew—the moment she knocked on the window while he tried to pop the slot.

She'd said something he totally missed. "What?"

"I said, what makes you think I'm seeing a doctor?"

"Look around you! Rather than retreating to a safe distance and calling the cops, you leapt on the car."

"*My* car."

"And now you're in the car, riding with a desperate criminal."

"*My* car with a desperate criminal."

"And you need new programming."

"What?"

"Never mind."

"I should have just let you take my car? Just stood back helplessly and let you have your way with me? With it?" she corrected herself, her face getting redder by the moment. "Well, fuck you!"

"Whoa," he muttered, taking a left at the light. She'd gone from annoying robot to screaming, red-faced psychotic. And it was sexy as hell.

"Fuck you if you thought I'd do that. I don't roll over for any man, and never a thief. So give up now, or I promise you, you'll be sorry."

"I already kind of am."

He pulled into a large Park 'n' Fly lot, put the Mustang in neutral, hit the parking brake, and got out.

After a moment, she got out, too.

"I give up," he said, raising his hands. "It's all yours. Thank you and good night."

He looked around the parking lot, seeing several nice candidates. Minnesota—land of the sleeping. It was so easy to snatch in this state. The only easier one? North Dakota.

She came around the side of the car to glare up at him. She was just the right size for a woman, in his opinion, about five foot seven; he could have comfortably rested his chin on her head. Not that he dared. Safer to comfortably rest his chin on a cobra.

"That's it? You've given up?"

He stopped raising his hands and handed her the keys. She was so surprised, she dropped them. He patiently bent down, scooped them out of the gravel, stood, and handed them over.

"So . . . so I get in and drive away?"

He gallantly held the door open for her.

Still, she stood there. "And just leave you here?"

"I'll find a ride," he said, straight-faced.

She chewed on her lower lip, which made it swell. Which made him want to chew on it. Which was annoying—business first. And chewing on anything belonging to the D.A.'s sister was a bad, bad, bad idea.

"No," she said at last. "I can't."

# DOING IT RIGHT

"Sure you can. Climb in, put it in first, stomp on the accelerator—that's the pedal on the right—"

"I'm aware of how to drive a stick, thank you."

"Well. 'Bye."

Still she stood there, looking up at him with an expression he couldn't read—surprise? Shock? Bewilderment? Helplessness?

*Don't.*

He took a step toward her.

*Bad idea, man.*

There was no room between them now.

*Dude, you will be so completely sorry.*

He cupped her—hot—face in his hands and eased his mouth to hers, touching her soft lips with his, then easing them apart with his tongue as he tasted her, touched her tongue with his, breathed in her scent, let his fingers plunge through her wild curls, testing their texture, tasting her mouth, her ripe, sweet, mouth, feeling the excruciating pain explode through his testicles and race up to his kidneys, watched her tip away from him as the gravel rushed to his face. The rocks should have hurt like hell but they felt like moss, and then nothing felt like anything, and he went bye-bye in his head.

# Chapter 4

"Tom, you've got to come *see*," Kat said urgently, waving her hands before his face. Her big brother ignored her, as was the purview of older brothers the world over, still chatting on his cell phone as he shrugged into his suit coat, shut down his computer, maneuvered his way around the stacks of legal files, and followed her out the door to the parking ramp.

"Yes—yes! Come on, you aren't really . . . you are? For God's sake, of course you need a bigger house—the governor's mansion wouldn't be big enough—What? Uh-huh. Other than take in more foster kids than Mia Farrow and Angelina Jolie put together, you—Yes? She did not—Well, tell her I'm keeping an eye on both of you . . ."

Kat noticed other women checking her brother out, not that she could blame them. Except for the tie—a nightmare of green spots on a barf-brown background—he was a good-looking man in his mid-thirties—dark blond hair cropped short all over, tall and athletic—he took pleasure in kicking Judge Kimmes's ass every week at racquetball—with the light blue eyes that were, except in her case, the Wechter trademark.

". . . she did? Oh boy. Didn't I tell you? I told you, you'll have your hands full. What is this, your third baby in how many—No! That's really pretty. Yeah, I have to—my sister's here and I've got to—Okay. Say hi to Kara for me. I'll talk to you later, Jared. Oh, hey, doc, it hurts when I do this. Yeah, yeah, don't do that. 'Bye."

Tom slapped his phone closed and looked at her. "What in the world is so important in the middle of a Friday afternoon? I've got cases to prep for and—"

"Deals to make, no doubt." She puffed a curl out of her face. Of all the days to forget a hair clip or a rubber band. "Come look what I've got." She looked around, but the police station was two blocks over—parking was lousy in Minneapolis on game nights. She'd been lucky to get this close to his office. "Maybe we should get a cop."

"Katherine Anne Wechter, what have you done now?" Her brother asked this in his thunder-court voice, the tone that made criminals cower and bailiffs grin and judges widen their eyes. His sister had heard it all her life, and it made her roll hers.

"Simmer down, D.A., which I've decided stands for Dickless Ass—"

"Don't say it." He looked around the parking

ramp. "Why in the world did you drag me to your—" He fell silent as he heard the furious thumping coming from his sister's trunk.

As they got closer to her Mustang, they could hear muffled commands—"Help! Police! Anybody! Kidnapping! Help! Call a fireman! Get the jaws of life!"

Kat whacked the trunk with her fist. "Quiet in there. You'll use up your oxygen and suffocate."

A furious volley of kicks, followed by—"You bitch! You . . . you sneaky kissing robotic weird nutso psychotic kidnapping whack job!"

Her brother's blond brows shot up and he tried to loom over her, another trick that had never worked. "Kissing?"

She waved it away. "It's probably the fumes. He's delirious."

"Kat, what have you done?" He asked this in the tone she liked best: the tone of a broken man. And he used her nickname, which he almost never did. The entire family, from her mother down to Great Uncle Daniel, hated her nickname. Leftovers from a bad night, they thought. Given to her by the Bad Man who tried to do things to her, him and his friends.

Her true name, she had secretly thought, from that night and forever more. A Kat, not a kitty to be coddled and petted. A Kat. *Kat*, complete with claws and teeth.

"I captured a car thief. Now you can arrest him."

"Arrest him? I'm not a cop, darling little slightly dim sister."

"Well, we're kind of flying by the seat of our pants."

"You captured a thief?" His brows crinkled together into one big blond angry eyebrow. "You actually grabbed a strange man and stuffed him into the trunk of your car and drove him to my office?"

*Whap-whap-whap* from the trunk. "She seduced me first! Vile betrayer!"

"Katherine . . ."

"Don't worry, Tom. You worry way too much. I had it all under control." She decided not to mention leaping onto the hood. Or much of what followed. She leaned forward and whispered, "I'll unlock it and you grab him while he's disoriented."

"Wait—"

*Click.* The trunk swung open. They both stared down at the addled thief, who had both hands clamped over his eyes. "Help!" he yelled. "Kidnappers afoot!"

"See?" Kat said triumphantly. It was too bad, because he was really a fabulous-looking man, but the law was the law—he had to go. "I got him. Now you get him."

Her brother had bent over to get a good look at the hardened thug. "Katherine . . ."

"I told you," she told the thief. "Crime doesn't pay. It's practically my family's motto." *My boring, staid, low-risk family.*

The thief's hands lowered slowly and he blinked painfully at them. "Other than my mother's funeral, this is possibly the worst day of my life."

Her brother was still staring. She wasn't surprised. The whole family coddled her, ever since The Thing That Happened When She Was A Teenager. Like she couldn't take care of herself— a woman in her late twenties! Like she couldn't handle anything some car thief yo-yo threw at her.

"Oh God, Katherine, Katherine, what have you done now?"

"Made the streets safer once again," she said, trying not to overdose on the triumph.

Her big brother was cringing inside his suit jacket, seeming to lose weight before her eyes. She was afraid, for a moment, that he was going to fall into the trunk with the car thief.

Finally, he asked, "Chester McNamara?" in a doom-laden voice.

The thief squinted at him. "Oh. Hi, Tom."

*!!!!!!!!*

She gasped like a landed trout, before managing to spit out, "You two know each other?"

"Detective McNamara, this is my sister, Katherine Wechter. Katherine, this is Detective McNamara."

She leaned against her car so as not to fall into the trunk.

# Chapter 5

"You are not."
"I am."
"No."
"Yes, I really very am."
She hid her face. "No."
"Yup."
"So I take it, your cover, she is blown," her brother said in an awful fake accent.

"I'm not sure. I was supposed to be at the shop with a lister, ah"—he squinted at his watch—"half an hour ago."

"A lister?" she couldn't help asking.

"It's an A-list of desirable cars to steal," Tom answered absently. "Bad guys put in orders just like you do when you order a car from a lot."

"And somebody wanted a Ford Mustang?"

"Sure," the thief—er, Chester—said. "Happens all the time."

"So when you said it was a matter of life and death . . ."

"Sure. Mine. I mean, if I don't show up, my cover's blown and they'll track me down and shoot me in the face. If I show up, they might figure out I'm an undercover cop and shoot me in the face. If—"

"Enough with the shooting in the face!" Kat realized she'd been cringing on her trunk and abruptly stood. "Okay. Let's figure this out."

Chester and Tom looked at each other, then at her. "This is police business, Katherine," her brother began in that so irritating tone. "You—"

"Kathhhhherrrrinnnnnne," Chester teased.

"Shut up, *Chester*. Staying away isn't an option?"

Her brother rubbed the throbbing vein between his eyes. Hee! She loved when that happened. "We're not having this conversation with a civilian."

"Hey, at least one of us isn't a scum-spewing lawyer."

"What did Mom tell you about that?" he whined.

"Baby."

"Risk-taker."

"Suit."

"Psycho."

"Uh, Wechter siblings? Simmer down." Chester was looking between them both with not a little wariness in his eyes. "I think we can safely say, due to your assault on a police officer and subsequent kidnapping of same—"

"You were *stealing* my *car*!"

"—that the case is fucked at any rate. *Capiche*?"

"All the lawful owners would have gotten their property back," her brother said in that snotty tone she despised. Her brother was born with a ramrod up his butt; she wondered how their mother managed to change his diapers. Hell, he probably changed them himself.

"There isn't anything you can do? And by the way, you can't cry kidnapping if you didn't show me I.D."

"She's on to us," Chester stage-whispered to her brother.

"Goddammit! Nine months of undercover down the drain because you picked my sister's car?"

"Hey, it was on the list."

"That make and model?"

"And the license plate."

Her brother scowled, obviously mulling that one over, when Kat piped up, "Well, let's give it to them."

"Absolutely not."

"You're going to chuck all that budget money down the drain? Oh, the voters'll *love* that."

Her brother cringed. "Leave that to me," he said with a complete lack of conviction.

"Where were you supposed to drop the car off?"

"Stop!" her brother screamed, his fair face flushing the color of a ripe beet.

"Chop shop in the warehouse district."

"What part of 'Stop!' are you not getting, Detective?"

"*I* don't work for you," she pointed out.

"You're not too big to spank," Thomas growled back.

She ignored him, as she had most of her life, and turned to Chester and his pea green eyes. "Well, how many can there be?"

"What?"

"Chop shops. I mean, this is Minneapolis. Hardly a hotbed of crime."

She slammed the trunk shut, snatched the keys out of the lock, and climbed into the driver's seat. She started the car, and glared at the two men who were gaping after her. "Well?" she demanded. "You coming?"

Her brother actually stamped his foot. "No."

"Uh."

"Chester. No."

"Uh . . . it might work."

"You'll both get a bullet in the face for your trouble."

"What is this obsession with bullets and faces?" Kat bitched.

"I said *might* work." Chester touched his mouth. "Ummm. How come you never mentioned you had a crazy gorgeous sister?"

"For obvious reasons, McNamara, and just forget it."

"And let her go out there alone? It's almost dark."

"At least let me—" But McNamara was gone, long legs scissoring into the passenger side. He put out a hand and gave Tom the—Was that the . . . ? Did he dare to . . . ? No, that was a *thumbs* up. "Cheer up!" he called as she squealed out of the parking space, ruffling her brothers three-hundred-dollar Men's Wearhouse suit. "We'll think of something."

"I'm telling Mom!" Thomas called after the Mustang, and she flashed its lights in saucy reply.

# Chapter 6

"I know why I'm doing this," Chester said, "but why in the world are you doing this? You're not a cop. You're a—What are you?"

"A boring rich person. No day job."

"Thus the sweet car."

"Thus." She took an illegal left and scooted up into the right-hand turn lane. "Warehouse district, coming up."

"So why are you doing this? I mean, any sane woman would have let me take her car. Especially a rich sane woman. But you kidnapped me and drove me to the D.A. And now you're driving me back to the bad guys."

"Thanks for the re-cap. Because I wasn't, you know, standing right there or anything."

"I've been working with your brother for over a year. He never mentioned anything about you. Specifically, I mean." Chess cringed as she squealed around a corner. She was—almost—a better driver. Certainly more reckless. "Just that his folks were still together and he had six brothers and sisters."

"Sheep," Kat muttered.

"What?"

"Sheep. They're very risk averse."

"You mean they're sane and sensible."

"Boring and overprotective."

"Well, rich people usually are."

"I'm the only one who's rich."

"How come?"

"Civil lawsuit in my favor," she replied shortly, neglecting to put on her turn signal as she took a right. "Tons of money I'll never use."

"And you're—" Bracing himself on the dashboard: "Yellow light yellow light *yellow fucking light!*"

"Will you calm down? How can an undercover cop have nerves of spaghetti?"

"Bad *guys* don't scare me."

She quirked a dark brow at him and he determinedly ignored the stiffening in his pants. His balls still throbbed, but in a much more interesting way. "How about bad girls?"

"Mmmmph."

"So it's Detective Chester—"

"Chess, please, if you love me."

"It's a little soon for—"

"Left, left, *left!*"

She swung left, ignored the squealing brakes behind her, and swung into the parking lot of a block-wide city garage.

"Okay," he panted, clutching his chest. "You stay

here. I'll tell them it took a while to find the car they wanted, but I've got it now. You'll—"

"I'm coming with."

"The hell."

"But I am."

"The. *Hell.*"

"Then why did you let me drive?"

"Because you've got the reflexes of a marmoset," he complained.

"Look, Chess, my days of sitting on the sidelines like a rabbit are *over*. You have a lot better chance of walking out there without getting shot if I'm some slut you picked up on the way."

"Why would I pick up some slut on the way?"

"Because crooks are stupid."

He acknowledged that with a silent nod. He'd lost track of how many busts had happened with the ease of closing a door, simply because the perp was, well, an idiot.

"You don't look like a slut."

She shook her hair until it stood out wildly in all directions, gypsy's hair. She reached into her purse, pulled out a slim silver tube, and glossed her mouth an even, glistening carmine red. She pulled off her sweater, revealing a black jogging bra. She wriggled out of her jeans, revealing workout leggings with lace cuffs in the same fuck-me red as her lipstick.

"How about now?" she asked, grinning at him in the gloom.

"Buh," he replied, or at least that's what he thought he said.

She jammed an apple-sized piece of gum into her mouth and began to masticate. "The final touch," she drooled with her mouth full.

Meanwhile, Chess had recovered his wits enough to get out, come around the front of the car, and open the door for her. She was wearing bronze-colored kitten heels which brought out the gold flecks in her black eyes—Wait a minute. Earlier he had thought her eyes had no color at all, and now they were, what? Sparkling?

"This is fucked up," he muttered.

She snapped her gum in reply.

"Your brother is going to lock me at the bottom of a cold, dark hole for the next fifty years."

She blew a bubble the size of her head, sucked it in, then clicked into the garage in her cute bronze shoes. "Hi!" she said. "Are you Manny's friends?"

There were several clangs as tools were dropped all over the garage.

# Chapter 7

*I* *am in love,* Chester McNamara, Detective Second Grade, thought, watching Kat's tight ass wiggle in front of him. *So, so in love. Not because of the killer bod. And I can overlook the annoying gum snapping. No, I'm in love because she kneed me in the nads, kidnapped me, ratted me out to the D.A., then relented and drove me to the pit of all evil to keep me from getting killed, which I probably will be anyway.*

Then: *Manny?*

Boss Jack, a willowy man with skin the color of cream cheese, a man who could have played professional basketball if he'd shown the slightest interest in anything but crime, ambled out of the cube of his office and approached them. "You're late."

"Sorry, boss."

"Not like you at all."

"I, uh . . ." He jerked a thumb at Kat, who was

cooing over a line of Michelins. "I ran into an old friend I haven't known very long."

Kat was running a hand over the dark tires. "They smell so rubbery!"

"You made a date you forgot about?" Boss Jack smiled, a warm, friendly smile which was usually the last thing a victim saw before the world exploded in brains and blood. "It's not like you to double book."

"Naw. A date I just—You know. Had to go for. I mean, right that minute." *A date I had no choice in. A terrifying, gorgeous date who kidnapped me.*

"I question your judgment in bringing her here." *That makes two of us.* "Why?" he duhhed.

"And these . . . What do you call these?" Kat was oohing. "They're so shiny!"

"Hubcaps," one of the mechanics piped up helpfully.

"Ummm." Boss Jack stroked his close-cropped beard—two shades darker than the white-blond hair on his head—and studied Kat, who was bent at the waist, peering into the pit. The mechanics were staring up at her cleavage, entranced. Then, "Manny?"

"Well. Had to tell her something."

Kat was waving down into the pit. "Hi, down there!"

From below, a cheerful chorus—"Hi, up there!" Other than stripping engines and moving parts out the door, Chess figured this was the most excitement these guys probably had in a year.

"You brought what I want?" Boss Jack continued.

"Huh?" Chess had been more than a little entranced himself. "Oh, the 'Stang! Yep, it's right outside."

"Not just any Mustang. *That* Mustang. Yes?"

"Sure." Chess didn't think much of the request at the time; sometimes people arranged to have their own cars stolen, or a relative's. That wasn't likely in Kat's case, but now that he had a chance to give it some thought, why would Boss Jack want Kat's car? She sure didn't want someone to take it, and he doubted her goody-goody family wished grand theft auto on her, either. As for her stick-in-the mud brother, he had the contacts, sure. But the motive? Nuh-uh.

"Very good," Jack continued. *Uh-oh,* Chess thought. *Better pay attention.* "At least you haven't lost all your faculties." Boss Jack motioned to a man loitering by the garage wall. "Bring in, ah, Manny's car, will you?"

"Aren't you scared the car will fall on you?" Kat asked the pit crew, absently—or artfully—twirling a curl around one long finger. She was bent over so far, Chess worried she might fall in herself.

"You've done well, Manny."

"Huh?"

"Seventeen cars in twelve days. And the only time you dropped off the radar was this afternoon."

"Yeah, but, boss . . ." He gestured as Kat squatted over the pit. "*Look* at her!"

"And you told her . . .?"

"That I was dropping a car off for a friend, and that we'd go out drinking after. She thinks the transmission's shot or something."

"You doubtless could have told her the fifth wheel was flat and she wouldn't have minded."

"Yeah, but . . . you get a look at her ass?"

Boss Jack grinned. Chester grinned back. And suddenly, he didn't want to be playing this game anymore. Fine, Kat had—probably—saved his life. Or at least the case, which he and her brother had been building for eleven months. But she was practically prostituting herself to do it, and that was just plain fucked up. God, if her brother could see her now, his entire head would pop like an enraged pimple.

The Mustang purred into the garage and, to Chess's dislike, the garage door ratcheted down right behind it. That was a small breach of protocol. Usually he just walked out the door. What was . . .

"This was . . . a special request. I'm very, very glad you were able to deliver . . . 'Manny.' "

"Yeah, well. Hooray for American ingenuity," he mumbled. He didn't like this. He didn't like this at all. And of course he had no back up, no badge, no gun. All he had was Kat, and all she had was—well, she had plenty, but he didn't think her jogging bra was bulletproof.

"If you and your . . . lady friend will just have a seat in my office, I'll get your wages." Boss Jack crossed the garage in three long-legged strides, grasped Kat's elbow, and lifted her to her feet. Startled, she snapped her gum in his face. He grimaced, bloodshot brown eyes narrowing, but didn't flinch.

"'S up?" she chewed.

"I owe your new friend some money, and then you two can dance the night away as far as I'm concerned."

"Okey-dokey," she said cheerfully. "Got somewhere I can freshen up?" She leaned toward Jack, snapped her gum in his ear even louder, ignored his flinch, then said, "I gotta pee something awful."

Boss Jack managed to keep a companionable arm around her shoulders while leaning as far away from her as possible. "There's a bathroom in my office. Manny, I believe you know the way."

He did know the way. He could even point out the bloodstains on the floor, covered in carpet though they were. He sighed, took Kat by the hand, and led her to the abattoir.

# Chapter 8

She bustled out of the small bathroom and plopped down on the couch beside Chess, who was chewing his lower lip and looking rather constipated.

"So, now what?"

He threw an arm around her shoulder, ignoring her squeak of surprise, and hauled her close enough so that his lips were tickling her ear. "The office is bugged."

"Well, duh," she whispered back.

"Audio and video. Don't look around."

"I wasn't going to."

She shifted her weight and slung a leg over his left thigh. He stiffened—she had no idea why, he certainly seemed like the touchy-feely type—and said, "What are you doing?"

"It's not going well, is it?" she breathed into his ear.

"Uh, no. I'm usually in and out of this place in about two minutes."

"Well. Better put on a good show."

"Is that Grape Bubblicious? Because I'm about to pass out from the fumes."

She stuck a finger in her mouth and pulled out the wad of gum. "Better?"

"No." He eyed her be-gummed finger warily. "What are you going to do—Mmph!"

Kiss him until he practically fell off the couch, that's what she was going to do. In half a second they were wrapped in each other's arms and he forgot about the gum as her mouth opened beneath his, as her hands groped and touched and teased, as he did a little groping of his own, as they sighed and gasped and wriggled on the couch.

Kat wasn't sure if the wild excitement she felt was because she was doing something extremely un-Wechter-like, because Chess was an amazing kisser, or because she knew someone—probably the tall creepy guy—was watching them. Whatever the reason, she'd gone from cool to flaming in five seconds, and was ready to rip Chester's pants off and jump him on the office floor, and never mind that the room stank of motor oil, and had a picture of Miss February—it was fall—on the wall.

"This is an excellent plan," Chester gasped, coming up for air, "but it's not really getting us anywhere."

"Shut up and kiss me some more."

"What are you, the black sheep of your family or something?"

"I'm the super-nova of black sheep. The black hole of black sheep."

He looked fascinated, trapped beneath her leg and twined in her arms as he was. "Why? What happened? Mix-up at the hospital?"

"It's a long story, and I come off really bad in it. Shouldn't we be making out more?"

"I was thinking of making for the back door," he mumbled in her ear, leaning in so close it looked, to a casual observer, as if he were nibbling on her earlobe. "This was a mistake all the way around. Jack's no one to fuck with."

"Neither am I," she said smugly. "You think my brother's bad?"

"I think your brother's a pussycat, comparably speaking."

"Ooooh, that made me horny all over again."

He laughed; he couldn't help it. The laughing cut off as the office door opened and Boss Jack stood framed in the doorway.

"Dum-dum-*dummmmmmm*," Kat hummed dramatically.

"I've got your wages," Jack lied politely. "So you can collect them and be on your way."

Neither of them moved. They just looked up at Jack from each other's arms. Finally, Chess managed, "Uh, great."

"Super great," Kat chirped. "Did you know it's not February anymore?"

He eyed her disheveled curls with distaste. "I prefer blondes."

"Hey," Chess said warningly.

"Both of you chill," Kat said. "Are we going or are we going? I'm bored out of my tits."

Both men made a concerted effort not to stare at her chest. "In just a few more moments. Follow me, please."

They did.

# Chapter 9

The first thing Chess noticed was how deserted the garage was. Most of the strippers/mechanics had left, leaving three thuglike gentlemen loitering near the Coke machine. As if enough alarm bells weren't ringing in his head, he suddenly wanted an Advil. And his service revolver.

"Do you recognize me?" Boss Jack asked Kat with alarming pleasantness.

"No."

"Something about the shape of my face? My mouth? The color of my eyes?"

"You look a little like my geometry teacher from tenth grade," she suggested, sounding so uninterested that Chess almost hugged her.

"I look," he said, "like my younger brother."

She sucked the gum off her finger and began masticating. "That's nice. Is he a tall weird skinny blond guy, too?"

"He's in jail."

"Uh-huh." She blew a bubble, popped it. "So?"

"Yeah," Chess said slowly, not liking this at all. "So?"

"So you testified against him. And they bitched him, so he's going to be in Stillwater for a while."

"Habitual offender," Chess muttered.

"I *know*," Kat snapped. "Oh. That brother."

If Boss Jack was waiting for alarm, or fear, he wasn't getting it. In fact, he sounded distinctly put out as he said, "It's all your fault he's locked up in a seventy-square-foot box."

"Oh, just *stop* it," Kat said, and Boss Jack jumped. Chess was keeping a wary eye on the thugs chugging Coke, but her tone made him snap his head around and stare at her. "Your brother? The innocent victim? My ass. He pulled me out of a party—pretended to be nice—and set me up to be gang-raped by his asshole buddies. That was almost ten years ago! If he's still in jail, it's not just for that and you know it. So, what? You figured out my license plate and sicced Chess on me?"

Chester silently groaned and fought the urge to slap his forehead. *Manny,* he mouthed.

She waved it away. "Forget it. He knows. The jig, as they say, is up. So, I'm here, Boss Jerk. What's the plan? Sic your thugs on me? Get revenge for your stupid little brother, who was so fucking dumb he dragged me out of a bar in front of thirty witnesses?"

"Kat," Chess growled, but he couldn't help grinning.

"Tracking you down was easy," Jack said, with the air of a man dying to tell his tale. "And you got reckless. Ever since you put my brother away, you take chances, you go your own way, you ignore good sense, and you think your shit doesn't stink."

"No," she said. "I just stopped being afraid."

"I knew if I sent Chester to get your car, you'd find a way to get it back. I assumed your cursed brother would help you, but I knew I'd see you again."

"A regular Nostrafuckingdamus, that's you."

"I didn't expect you to walk into my garage this very night, but that's all right. The gods are finally smiling on *my* family for a change."

"Wrong again, Jacko. Did you really think we came here alone?"

"You did. My men checked the perimeter."

"Oh, the idiots with a combined IQ of sixty? Those men?"

"You—" He took a step forward, and so did Kat. Chess got ready to jump between them—possibly losing an eye or a limb in the process—when the garage door began to beep and inch upward.

Boss Jack whirled on the men chugging pop. "I thought you locked it."

"We did," one of them said, and belched lightly.

"The lock's being bypassed," Kat said. "Duh."

"But the cops can't come in here without—"

"Who said anything about cops?" Kat rolled her eyes. "How did you get to be the boss again? I know you didn't have to take an intelligence test or anything."

The door slowly ratcheted up, revealing slim legs and hips in dark jeans, a dark sweatshirt, a blonde with a ponytail lying over her left shoulder, one so long it trailed almost to her waist, a beautiful woman holding the hand of a small boy who looked about four.

"This is a chop shop," she explained like a schoolteacher, stepping into the garage. "It's where bad guys cut up cars and sell them for scrap."

"This is another thing not to tell Daddy about," the boy said, "right?"

"You got it, kiddo."

Boss Jack actually blanched. "You're out of the business," he said. "You're a civilian now."

"Yeah, well. I like to take tours on the wild side now and again. And the kid's seen all the museums in town."

"A.A.?" Chess gasped. "I thought you were an urban legend!"

"Hey," one of the thugs whined. "Nobody said we had to go up against her."

"So don't," the blonde said, eyeing them coldly.

"Everybody stay put," Boss Jack ordered.

"Boss, she took down the Minnesota Mafia!"

"She did not, she only took down the head mobster. Stay."

"I think you better go," the little boy said, almost apologetically. He had his mother's eyes, and brown hair which, under the fluorescents, showed deep red highlights. His nose was sprinkled with freckles. "Otherwise you'll get beat up and it'll just be a big mess."

"Hush, David," the blonde said absently, and the boy hushed.

Kat snapped her fingers with delight. "My brother called you! He's been keeping in touch all this time."

"He had this silly idea that you might rush headlong into trouble—again—and might need me to save your ass. Again."

"Mom."

"An ass is a donkey. It's not a swear word."

"*Mom.*"

"Cram it, kid."

Boss Jack, the idiot, was actually rubbing his hands together, which made a rasping sound that set Chester's teeth on edge. "Both of the twats who put my brother in a cell, here under my roof at the same time. You think she's here for you? I tell you, she's here for me."

"Oh, blow me," A.A. said indifferently.

"Mom!"

"Like a fan. You know, to cool off."

David rolled his eyes, looking uncannily like his mother as he did so. "Mom, I hate it when you treat me like a kid."

"You are a kid. Okay, granted, you've got twenty IQ points on me, but I've got three feet and a hundred pounds on you."

"Might makes right?"

"Something like that."

Boss Jack pointed a skeletal finger at them. "It was a mistake to bring your son here. The last thing he'll see will be your blood puddling on the—"

The boy yawned. Then apologized "Sorry. It's past my bedtime."

"Don't apologize to the bad guy," A.A. ordered. "You'll do more than apologize."

"Why do I have the feeling this isn't the first lair of evil your mother's brought you to?" Chess asked.

David shrugged. "She had a yucky childhood. She wants me to know what the bad guys look like."

"If we could keep our attention on the matter at hand," Boss Jack practically shouted, clearly annoyed. "When my men and I are through with you—"

"What men?" David asked.

Boss Jack looked. They all looked. The thugs, doubtless calculating the odds of an unfair fight in their favor, and disliking them, had crept out the back.

"Never mind," Boss Jack said, going pale but recovering. "I can handle you myself. I've been waiting for years to—Yurrrgggghhhh!" He went paler—if possible—clutched himself between his legs, and dropped to the concrete floor like a sack of flour dropped from a great height.

Kat nudged him over on his back with her foot, and kicked him again, this time across the chin. Boss Jack's eyes rolled up, but didn't close.

"And there's plenty more where that came from," A.A. said. Then, to Kat, "I'm supposed to save you, honey."

"Not this time. It's very nice to see you again, by the way. You kind of vanished after the last time."

"I kind of hid from your brother for a decade or so."

"And who could blame you?" Kat said cheerily. "I could have told you he was just looking for a chance to help you out."

"Oh, sure, *now* it comes out."

David let go of his mother's hand, crossed the room, and peered down at Jack's pupils. "He's out," the boy announced.

"His eyes are open," Chess said doubtfully.

"It doesn't mean anything. My dad's a doctor, and he says . . . Anyway, I don't think he has a concussion, but that looked like a pretty hard kick to me. And the blow to the testes didn't help, either."

Chess stared wonderingly down at the kid. "How old are you?"

"Four."

"Oh my God."

"Uh-huh." The boy nodded. "Mom says I'll be formidable." He hesitated, then smiled his mother's smile, sweet and sunny. "Don't tell Daddy, though."

# Chapter 10

"That was so . . ." Kat groped for the word.

"Anticlimactic?" Chess suggested.

"Well, yeah. I mean, I still have nightmares about those guys. And if I'd ever thought that the guy's big brother's been thinking about how to get me all these years—Jesus, I probably would have slit my wrists ten years ago."

Chester laughed.

"Well, okay, maybe not. Still. You worry about something and you take self-defense classes and you try to make yourself be brave even when you're scared to death and then there's this big showdown and it's over in about ten seconds. I mean, jeez." Pouting, she slouched back in the passenger seat. "I can't believe my brother told her to come get me."

"He was just looking out for you. I don't think he could have sent a million cop cars in with screaming sirens. Somebody was bound to get shot."

"Yeah, yeah." She waved the prospect of imminent death away with a dainty hand. "So, now what?"

"Now I drive you home."

"Oh." She tried not to sound disappointed.

"And we'll get married soon."

"Oh?"

"Sure," he said casually. "I sort of fell in love with you a couple hours ago."

"You did? You did not. Really? You did?" Now she sounded like an idiot schoolgirl, delighted over a first crush, but she couldn't help it. She liked everything about him. Shit, she had liked him when she thought he was a car thief.

"For crying out loud, Kat, what's not to love? You waltzed into danger chewing grape bubble-gum, for God's sake. You beat the shit out of the bad guy. The Avenging Angel came out of retirement to save your ass, not that you needed it, and you've obviously got some seriously powerful friends. Plus, you've got a killer bod and you kiss like the devil."

"Kissed the devil, have you?" she teased.

"Only tonight." He breathed in. "God, I love the smell of leather. And your car. And you."

"Pull over," she said suddenly. They were driving past one of the lakes in Eagan, and with the fall chill in the air, the parking lots for the beaches were deserted.

Knowing exactly what she had in mind—and

thanking God for it—he yanked the wheel to the left, not bothering with a turn signal, screeched to a halt, and slammed the car into first. Then shut it off and dropped the keys on the mat as she grabbed him around the collar and hurled them both—somehow; he outweighed her by forty pounds—into the backseat.

"I wouldn't . . . exactly . . . call this . . . roomy," he gasped, pulling and tugging and tearing at her clothes, as she groped and fought his shirt and jeans.

"Shut . . . up."

"Just . . . saying."

Her thighs were the color of alabaster under the harsh parking lot lights, and her black hair tumbled over his face, his throat, and he breathed deep of her perfume, her own special scent, and the leather—*don't forget the leather*—and oh God, he loved cars and he loved women, especially this woman and this car, and oh God, she was touching him, no, grabbing him, tugging at him and stroking, and he snatched her hands away and said, "We'll be done before we get started if you keep that up."

"So?" she replied saucily, black eyes gleaming, and somehow she wriggled around so he was on top and she was bracing one foot on the passenger seat headrest and the other on the top of the backseat, and he was pushing into her, shoving into her, and she gasped and wriggled closer, and at first he was worried he was hurting her but she was squirming and groaning beneath him and it was a sound any man could recognize—the sound of wanting, the sound of urgent lust.

She pulled him closer, clung to him as he thrust, as she met his every stroke, as her ankles crossed behind his back to hold him closer, as she shivered beneath him and whispered his name, and that was it, that was all, he was done, and collapsed over her in an ungainly heap.

"Oh, *that's* sexy," she gasped, half her breath gone.

"Shut up," he groaned.

"I've never done it in a backseat before."

"Because you're such a goody-goody," he smirked.

"Not anymore. Not for years and years."

He smelled her hair, and got another intoxicating whiff of leather. She shifted until she was spearing him with her black gaze. "Tell the truth," she said. "Do you love me because of my car, or do you love your car because of me?"

"Uh . . ." Too late, he realized it was a fatal pause.

"Well, I'm not going to marry you then," she said with terrifying finality.

"What?" He would have leapt off her in a panic, but there was nowhere to go.

"Nope. Everybody in my family gets married and settles down."

"Uh-huh. I'm not sure your family will approve of me."

"Eh. You're a cop."

"A scruffy undercover cop who spends way more time pretending to be a bad guy than trying to be a good guy."

"Yeah," she said, satisfaction unmistakable in her voice.

"You're still marrying me."

"Nope." She paused, long enough for his heart to stop. "But we'll date for the rest of our lives."

"Date?" he cried, outwardly aggrieved, inwardly relieved.

"Well, you know. Until you knock me up."

"Oh, your family's gonna *love* that."

She laughed so hard, she nearly dislodged him onto the floor. "Argh, stop it! I'm slipping!"

"You're damned right you're slipping," she said, still giggling. "You slipped the minute I put you on citizen's arrest."

"Marry me."

"Date me."

"Done," they said in unison, and the long struggle to get back into their clothes began.

*Hello, Gorgeous!*

**They Want Her To Save The World. As If.**

One minute I'm out with my sorority sisters; the next there's a terrible accident (beyond my friend Stacey's outfit) and I'm waking up in some weird clinic transformed into a human cyborg—with a mission: to stop evil and stuff. Uh, hello? I've got a beauty salon to run.

Granted, it is cool to run faster than a Ford Mustang when I need to, even if it's totally hard on my shoes. But then I have to bring in another human cyborg on the run? One who happens to be male, totally gorgeous, smart, funny—and, um, his "enhancements"?—as if!

*Drop Dead, Gorgeous!*

**Fast. Powerful. Deadly. With Bitchin' Highlights.**

Ah, weddings—every single woman's reminder that she'll probably die alone, covered in cat hair and dressed in unflattering sweatpants. And as far as bad wedding experiences go, my friend Stacy's could take the cake. 1) I'm dateless 2) I'm a bridesmaid, and 3) Someone just attempted to whack the groom (known, no kidding, as The Boss) in the middle of the ceremony. Whoa... hang on. I might not relish reception food or doing the Electric Slide, but anyone who tries to ruin a girlfriend's big day by bumping off her true love will have to go through me first.

So now I, assistant hairdresser Jenny Branch, am helping to hunt down a real-life bad guy, and the prime suspect is Kevin Stone, who claims to be working undercover for a group called Covert Ops Protection. Riiiight. All of this is hard to believe— my new role as spy-in-training, the fact that I'm surrounded by people with freaky superhuman powers, and most of all, the way that this unbelievably sexy villain/double agent/whatever Kevin is makes every (and I mean every) nerve-ending tingle the second he comes into view... and it appears to be mutual. Living with flying bullets and constant danger is a long way from sweeping up hair at the end of the day. But if it means being around Kevin, a girl could get used to it . . .

MaryJanice Davidson's sequel to *Hello, Gorgeous!* is a nonstop thrill-ride of secret agents, wickedly seductive superspies, and deadly weapons, where a fearless, funny heroine and an irresistible hero could find themselves saving the universe . . . and setting each other's worlds on fire . . .

*The Royal Treatment*

In a world nearly identical to ours, the North won the Civil War, Ben Affleck is the sexiest man alive, and Russia never sold Alaska to the U.S. Instead, Alaska is a rough, beautiful country ruled by a famously eccentric royal family, and urgently in need of a bride for the Crown Prince. But they have no idea what they're in for when they offer the job to a feisty commoner . . . a girl who's going to need . . .

*The Royal Treatment*

**The Princess-To-Be Primer,**

Or, Things I've Learned Really Quick, As Compiled by Her Future Royal Highness—Yeah, Whatever—Christina. That's me.

1. Telling jokes you picked up from the guys on the fishing boat doesn't go over really well at a fancy ball.
2. Must learn to curtsy, stifle burps, and tell the difference between a salad fork and a fruit knife.
3. Must not keep thinking about Prince David's amazing eyes, lips, hands, shoulders, uh . . . wait, can I start over?

4. Becoming a princess is a lot harder than it looks.
5. Falling in love is a whole lot easier . . .

In this dazzling, delightfully wacky tale from Mary-Janice Davidson, a tough commoner and a royal prince are about to discover that who they truly are . . . and what they desperately desire . . . may both be closer than they ever dreamed . . .

*The Royal Pain*

In a world nearly identical to ours, the North won the Civil War, Ben and JLo got married, and everyone dresses well to attend the Grammys. Oh, and Russia never sold Alaska to the U.S. Instead, Alaska is a rough, beautiful country ruled by a famously eccentric royal family, including oldest daughter, Princess Alexandria, whose acid wit and bad case of insomnia have turned her into a tabloid darling, a palace problem, and overall . . .

## The Royal Pain

Marine biologist Dr. Shel ("Never Sheldon") Rivers has a problem. Some princess expects him to wait on her, hand and dimpled foot. His boss is taken with the royal redhead—brunette, whatever, it's not like he keeps track of that stuff—and nobody realizes that he just wants to be left alone in his lab. All alone. All the time. Weekends, holidays . . . it's all good.

Now here's Miss Royalpants, insisting that he escort her around the marine institute, explain what he's doing, kiss her until her toes curl . . . no, wait, that was his idea. She's not even apologetic about being born into a royal family! Says it's his problem to overcome, not hers. Which leaves him with one option: to kiss her again. And again. And . . .

So she's nothing like he expected. In fact, Dr. Rivers can see that this fantastic, exasperating woman has problems no princess should ever have to deal with. And he has an idea to help her get some much-needed sleep. Of course, it involves getting very, very tired beforehand, but if she's up to it, then so is he . . .

In this delightfully madcap sequel to *The Royal Treatment,* the Baranov family is back and as unpredictable as ever, and a prickly princess and cranky Ph.D. are about to discover that love conquers attitude every time . . .

*The Royal Mess*

In a world nearly identical to ours, the North won the Civil War, flannel is the new bling, and Russia never sold Alaska to the U.S. Instead, Alaska is a beautiful, rough-and-tumble country ruled by a famously eccentric royal family who put the fun back in dysfunctional. And the tabloid darlings are about to get more ink once the King's "royal oats" come back in the form of a surprise princess, landing them all in, well . . .

**The Royal Mess**

Jeffrey Rodinov is descended from one of the oldest families in Alaska, and a Rodinov has been protecting a Baranov for generations. It's a job Jeffrey takes VERY seriously. Six feet four inches, 220 fatless lbs., black hair, and blue eyes; weapon of choice: the 9 mm Beretta. In a pinch? His fists. IQ: 157. (Yes, crossword puzzle, in ink, just after taking out the guy behind you. No thanks necessary.) No one ever sees Jeffrey Rodinov coming, and no one—not even a mouthy, illegitimate princess—is going to keep him from playing bodyguard when his king decrees it.

Right. But no Rodinov ever had to protect Princess Nicole Krenski. Her credentials? Hunting guide in the Alaskan wilderness. Smart. Stubborn bordering on exasperating. Five-seven. Blue eyes. Very kissable mouth. Very kissable neck, back, legs, wrists, earlobes. The lady says she doesn't need a bodyguard, but that's where she's wrong. Someone needs to watch her and show her the royal ropes (and cuffs . . . and scarves . . .). Someone who can make her feel like a queen—in and out of bed. And that's a job Jeffrey Rodinov takes very seriously as well . . .

# Books by Bestselling Author
# Fern Michaels

| | | |
|---|---|---|
| ___The Jury | 0-8217-7878-1 | $6.99US/$9.99CAN |
| ___Sweet Revenge | 0-8217-7879-X | $6.99US/$9.99CAN |
| ___Lethal Justice | 0-8217-7880-3 | $6.99US/$9.99CAN |
| ___Free Fall | 0-8217-7881-1 | $6.99US/$9.99CAN |
| ___Fool Me Once | 0-8217-8071-9 | $7.99US/$10.99CAN |
| ___Vegas Rich | 0-8217-8112-X | $7.99US/$10.99CAN |
| ___Hide and Seek | 1-4201-0184-6 | $6.99US/$9.99CAN |
| ___Hokus Pokus | 1-4201-0185-4 | $6.99US/$9.99CAN |
| ___Fast Track | 1-4201-0186-2 | $6.99US/$9.99CAN |
| ___Collateral Damage | 1-4201-0187-0 | $6.99US/$9.99CAN |
| ___Final Justice | 1-4201-0188-9 | $6.99US/$9.99CAN |
| ___Up Close and Personal | 0-8217-7956-7 | $7.99US/$9.99CAN |
| ___Under the Radar | 1-4201-0683-X | $6.99US/$9.99CAN |
| ___Razor Sharp | 1-4201-0684-8 | $7.99US/$10.99CAN |
| ___Yesterday | 1-4201-1494-8 | $5.99US/$6.99CAN |
| ___Vanishing Act | 1-4201-0685-6 | $7.99US/$10.99CAN |
| ___Sara's Song | 1-4201-1493-X | $5.99US/$6.99CAN |
| ___Deadly Deals | 1-4201-0686-4 | $7.99US/$10.99CAN |
| ___Game Over | 1-4201-0687-2 | $7.99US/$10.99CAN |
| ___Sins of Omission | 1-4201-1153-1 | $7.99US/$10.99CAN |
| ___Sins of the Flesh | 1-4201-1154-X | $7.99US/$10.99CAN |
| ___Cross Roads | 1-4201-1192-2 | $7.99US/$10.99CAN |

## *Available Wherever Books Are Sold!*
Check out our website at **www.kensingtonbooks.com**

# Romantic Suspense from
# Lisa Jackson

| | | |
|---|---|---|
| **See How She Dies** | 0-8217-7605-3 | $6.99US/$9.99CAN |
| **Final Scream** | 0-8217-7712-2 | $7.99US/$10.99CAN |
| **Wishes** | 0-8217-6309-1 | $5.99US/$7.99CAN |
| **Whispers** | 0-8217-7603-7 | $6.99US/$9.99CAN |
| **Twice Kissed** | 0-8217-6038-6 | $5.99US/$7.99CAN |
| **Unspoken** | 0-8217-6402-0 | $6.50US/$8.50CAN |
| **If She Only Knew** | 0-8217-6708-9 | $6.50US/$8.50CAN |
| **Hot Blooded** | 0-8217-6841-7 | $6.99US/$9.99CAN |
| **Cold Blooded** | 0-8217-6934-0 | $6.99US/$9.99CAN |
| **The Night Before** | 0-8217-6936-7 | $6.99US/$9.99CAN |
| **The Morning After** | 0-8217-7295-3 | $6.99US/$9.99CAN |
| **Deep Freeze** | 0-8217-7296-1 | $7.99US/$10.99CAN |
| **Fatal Burn** | 0-8217-7577-4 | $7.99US/$10.99CAN |
| **Shiver** | 0-8217-7578-2 | $7.99US/$10.99CAN |
| **Most Likely to Die** | 0-8217-7576-6 | $7.99US/$10.99CAN |
| **Absolute Fear** | 0-8217-7936-2 | $7.99US/$9.49CAN |
| **Almost Dead** | 0-8217-7579-0 | $7.99US/$10.99CAN |
| **Lost Souls** | 0-8217-7938-9 | $7.99US/$10.99CAN |
| **Left to Die** | 1-4201-0276-1 | $7.99US/$10.99CAN |
| **Wicked Game** | 1-4201-0338-5 | $7.99US/$9.99CAN |
| **Malice** | 0-8217-7940-0 | $7.99US/$9.49CAN |

*Available Wherever Books Are Sold!*
Visit our website at **www.kensingtonbooks.com**

# More by Bestselling Author
# Hannah Howell